Weekly Reader

Children's Book Club

EDUCATION CENTER • COLUMBUS 16, OHIO

Presents

Ojibway Drums

by MARIAN W. MAGOON

Illustrated by LARRY TOSCHIK

OJIBWAY DRUMS

MARIAN W. MAGOON

Illustrated by LARRY TOSCHIK

LONGMANS, GREEN AND CO.

NEW YORK • LONDON • TORONTO

1955

LONGMANS, GREEN AND CO., INC.
55 FIFTH AVENUE, NEW YORK 3

LONGMANS, GREEN AND CO. LTD.
6 & 7 CLIFFORD STREET, LONDON W 1

LONGMANS, GREEN AND CO.
20 CRANFIELD ROAD, TORONTO 16

OJIBWAY DRUMS

PUBLISHED SIMULTANEOUSLY IN THE DOMINION OF CANADA BY
LONGMANS, GREEN AND CO., TORONTO

FIRST EDITION

WEEKLY READER
Children's Book Club
Edition, 1955

LIBRARY OF CONGRESS CATALOG CARD NUMBER 55-6730

Printed in the United States of America
American Book–Stratford Press, Inc., New York

Special Notice to Book Club Members

★ This book is a selection of the WEEKLY READER CHILDREN'S BOOK CLUB. It was chosen for you by the Editors and Selection Committee of *My Weekly Reader*, the most famous school newspaper in the world.

Members of the WEEKLY READER CHILDREN'S BOOK CLUB receive six or more exciting books during the year — including one or more Free Bonus Books upon joining. They also receive a Membership Certificate, Club Bookmarks and regular Book Club Bulletins.

We hope you enjoy this book and that you will tell your friends about the WEEKLY READER CHILDREN'S BOOK CLUB. They will want to become members, too!

WEEKLY READER

Children's Book Club

EDUCATION CENTER, COLUMBUS 16, OHIO

Contents

Illustrations

Ojibway Drums

CHAPTER 1

Iroquois Drums

LITTLE HALF SKY ate too much boiled fish and wild rice for supper. Right now his stomach ached. When he had kept passing up his birchwood bowl to his mother, Flying Cloud, she had filled it, saying, "Twelve-year-old boys have hollow legs."

He wiggled around on his bearskin spread on the floor. Just above him on a little platform his father, his mother, and his little sister were sleeping. How he wished he would hurry and grow up. Some day he would be able to eat as much as his father and say, "Oongh ondjita—this hits the spot." Now however, even the thought of anything to eat made his stomach flip-flop, but he knew that no Indian boy who is almost ready to fast and find his manito, his spirit, on Dreamers' Rock should give in to a little stomach pain.

Just as soon as this Month of the Sturgeon was over and the Month of Indian Corn came, he would learn what animal was to be his life-long helper. He could then take his place in the Great Feast. He would sing about his manito and dance to the drum and rattle. Perhaps some day he would wear the feathers of the golden eagle in his headdress just as his father, Crashing Thunder, did. Oh, if time would hurry!

To forget his stomachache he tried to put his mind on

something else. How proud he would be to carry a medicine bundle. He'd sit in the Ojibway Council, too. He would paint himself red and yellow and black and go out against the Sioux, or Dacotahs, or Iroquois. His grandfather, Footsteps of the Bear, had often said that the Iroquois were the worst enemies the Ojibway had. Footsteps of the Bear knew, for he had been chief before his son, Crashing Thunder.

He often told Half Sky, "I've seen too many moons to lead a war party any longer." Half Sky sometimes wondered at this, because Footsteps of the Bear, though ninety years old, had black hair and flashing eyes. Not a creature roamed Birch Island but Grandfather could make a snare that would catch it.

Half Sky could not go to sleep. He decided to play his listening game. Birch Island village seemed quiet enough, but Half Sky knew it was filled with sounds. He'd try to see how many he could hear and if he could tell what made them.

Ah-o-o-o! Ah-o-o-o!

"Oh, that's a loon." Half Sky, like every other Indian boy, knew the loon.

Chonk, chonk, chonk.

"Another easy one. A porcupine gnawing away on some bark near the cabin. He's looking around for salt."

Hurum, hurum, hurum, kerchug.

"Bull frogs." He wondered where those frogs were. He wouldn't mind eating some frogs' legs. They'd make a good meal some time. Cooked next to the birchwood fire and served with his mother's corn bread . . . His stomach growled. No more thinking of food, he decided.

Slap, slap, slap.

The water around Birch Island was beginning to talk. Half Sky knew how it came rolling in from the big lake, past Quartz Rock, past Bell Rocks, whose deep tones warned the Ojibways of danger, past the high flat island where the otters sunned themselves. Then with a swishing roar it crashed against the rocky point of Birch Island.

Whoosh, whoosh, whoosh.

The wind that made the big lake talk was sighing like a giant among the pines.

Hiss! Like a swish of a spruce rope a sound cut the night. Whoo—whoo—whoo.

"The big owl, the horned one," Half Sky said to himself. "He can imitate anything. He's hunting tonight. The rabbits better look out."

A faint clitter-clatter, clitter-clatter puzzled him. "What's that?" He sat up. "That's a new noise." He listened intently, then he laughed. "Why, it's only Crow Tongue. She's the funniest squaw on Birch Island. Always hungry, always snooping, she prowls around nights." After a while he heard her sneak off.

Tired of the sound game, he began to feel sleepy. He turned on his side and wriggled about; he found his head was off his bearskin, and his ear rested on the dirt floor. Just for fun he'd listen to what went on under the island. Crow Tongue was always telling of the huge misshapen spirits, Bad Matchi Manito's helpers, evil ones that live underground and . . . But what was that he was hearing?

Boom, boom, boombo, boom! Dum, dum, dummity, dum!

Oh, no. It couldn't be. But it was! War drums. Half Sky knew the sound of war drums. These weren't Ojibway, for his tribe was at peace. Ojibways loved peace. All they asked was to catch whitefish, harvest the wild rice, hunt the moose, deer, and bear, pick blueberries . . .

Boom, boom, boombo, boom! Dum, dum, dummity, dum!

On and on and on the sound throbbed. "Iroquois war drum, that's what it is." Half Sky wondered whether he ought to wake his father. Could it be that Matchi Manito's imps were beating out the Iroquois war song? Could it be? Hadn't Grandfather Footsteps of the Bear related how once a ten-year-old boy, guided by his manito, had led a war party?

All the while Half Sky was thinking whether to wake his father, he was listening to this strange drumming from afar. His father never made fun of him; he'd risk waking him. He crept over toward Crashing Thunder. Wriggling along the floor, he tried to get near enough to touch his father without waking his mother.

He had almost reached the sleeping platform when he heard, "What is it, Little Half Sky?"

The boy froze. All he could think was, I've been so clumsy that I awoke him. How ashamed I am!

"Speak."

Half Sky seldom heard his father use that tone. For a moment he was afraid. "I—I thought I heard something."

Crashing Thunder sat up. So did Flying Cloud.

"What did you hear, Half Sky?"

At least he doesn't call me *Little* Half Sky, the boy thought and gained courage enough to say, "Drums, Iroquois drums. I heard them."

"Iroquois drums? How do you know they are Iroquois drums?"

Flying Cloud drew in her breath sharply.

"Grandfather Footsteps of the Bear taught me the Iroquois war-drum song."

"Where did you hear them?"

"Right here on the floor. I had my ear down on the dirt. Here, you listen."

Crashing Thunder slid off his platform and laid his ear to the ground. For a long time he listened. Finally he sat up. "I don't hear one thing," he said slowly. "I don't believe you did. You must have been dreaming—but I can't say I like your dream."

Half Sky said nothing. At least his father believed he had not made up his story entirely.

"Let's have something to eat," Crashing Thunder said to Flying Cloud.

She nodded. "But," she said, "remember Half Sky has the gift of keen ears. You know the dream I had before he was born. I can still see how that big deer looked at me when he told me I'd have a son who would have the keenest sense of hearing of anyone ever born. Then the deer licked my hand. If Half Sky says he heard Iroquois war drums, he heard them."

Since it was a warm night, Flying Cloud decided to use the outside cooking fire. She lifted the skin flap of the birch-bark cabin and walked out. She blew up the embers of the fire and put on more birch wood. She reached into the mohuk or pail where she had put some corn meal that she had pounded in the mortar. Taking out two handfuls, she deftly mixed the meal with water, flapped the dough on a thin sheet of copper and set it up slantwise on the ashes so it faced the fire. She reached for the clay cooking pot that she had left almost half full of boiled fish.

"I know I left more fish than this. It's those thieving porkies. But I wonder how porkies could lift off the lid and put it on again? I put a piece of a broken cooking pot over the boiled fish." She was sputtering to herself.

"Crashing Thunder, my husband," she called, "you or Half Sky must do something about these porcupines. They are nuisances. They are too smart for me."

Half Sky giggled when he thought of what Flying Cloud would say if she knew of Crow Tongue's stealing fish. When two squaws like Flying Cloud and Crow Tongue begin to argue . . . No, he wouldn't say a word about Crow Tongue.

"I don't want anything to eat," Half Sky said.

"I shouldn't think you would," Flying Cloud answered. "I wondered how you slept with so much in your stomach, but I thought, He is just like his father, can eat any time, and besides he has hollow legs." She laughed.

"Not hollow head, though," Crashing Thunder added.

Flying Cloud pretended she did not hear. "What a man your father is—eats all the time," she began. Half Sky knew that his mother loved to cook and was happiest when Crashing Thunder gobbled up everything and then boomed out, "Oongh ondjita, enough."

She turned the tin of dough so the back was toward the fire. After a few minutes, she turned it again and tapped it with her knuckle. "It's done," she said. She broke off a big chunk of the hot bread and set it before her husband along with his wooden bowl filled with the boiled fish and corn soup.

He stuffed a big piece of bread into his mouth and chewed

loudly, pausing only to ladle up enormous spoonfuls of the soup. "Oongh ondjita—this is my dish, my dear wife."

Half Sky watched him admiringly. Crashing Thunder said, "Well, I guess that will last until breakfast," and beckoned his son to him.

"Half Sky, go to the tepees at the point of the island and ask each head of the family to come here to a council. I will take the end of the island, and we'll ask Footsteps of the Bear to notify those living in the middle. Go quickly, before the men get away fishing or hunting."

Crashing Thunder did not need to say hurry. Half Sky knew a council was important. In the grayness of dawn he ran toward the rocky point and almost collided with a boy, who called out:

"Hello, you dirty skunk. What are you doing up so early?"

"Hey, Big Face," Half Sky answered and hurried on. At any other time he would have retorted, "Hello, you stinking fish. Don't you know you're dead? Go bury yourself." This morning Half Sky felt grown up. He had business to do. Big Face opened his eyes wide as Half Sky raised the skin curtain that hung over Sparrow Hawk's doorway.

"Nind ubimin. Nind ubimin—we are at home, come in," called Big Face's father.

Half Sky entered and said, "Crashing Thunder wonders whether you can come to his house right away." As he turned to go, he remembered his manners and came back to say, "Sparrow Hawk, I am happy to see the Great Spirit has given you another day."

Sparrow Hawk nodded, and Half Sky ran on. At tepee after tepee he gave the same message. Finally he met his father and grandfather at the chief's round-domed house. Only a chief has a high round-roofed house, Half Sky knew, and he understood why: a tepee would not be large enough to hold all the warriors and older men his father had asked to the council.

As he stood outside the house, watching the men arrive and go inside, Half Sky was proud of being an Ojibway. Every man was of proven courage and had shown bravery in battle. They had wisdom.

"As I said to you before, when you were too scared to answer, 'Hello, you dirty skunk'." A voice behind him took Half Sky's thoughts from the council. He whirled around toward Big Face.

"You want to make something of it?" Half Sky asked.

"Fight. Fight. Fight!" yelled Crow Tongue. Her voice, shrill and raucous as the bird she was named after, brought boys, girls, and squaws on the run. They formed a circle around Half Sky and Big Face.

"Make his face bigger than it is, Half Sky," advised one boy. "Go make him eat skunk."

"He's only *Little* Half Sky," yelled another. "Make him littler."

Everyone took sides. Several wanted to bet on the outcome. Girls screamed. Dogs barked. Squaws giggled.

"Fight. Fight. Fight! Go on and fight," Crow Tongue taunted. "I don't think you know how. What do you think we're all waiting for?"

Suddenly the skin covering the doorway of the Council House was pushed aside and Crashing Thunder appeared. He said nothing but beckoned to Half Sky, who followed him inside the house.

"Yah, yah, yah," Big Face began but as he caught a glimpse of the men inside and saw the expressions on their faces, he backed away. "Now what's up?" he asked.

"He's a chicken, that's what he is," Crow Tongue answered Big Face. "Chicken, chicken, chicken. Here, chick, chick!"

"Oh, keep still," Big Face said. "There'll be time for a fight later, Crow Tongue. Something is happening. The men inside there looked just like—well, big stones."

Crow Tongue stared at him, and finally picked up her white splint basket and went out to look for wild potatoes. The other women went back to cutting up fish to put in the corn soup. "I wouldn't have left my tanning if I'd known there would be no fight," a fat squaw remarked.

Gradually the boys went off to practice with their bows and arrows, and the girls sat down to shaping clay cooking pots.

Flying Cloud, however, did not go on with her corn pounding. She sat on a log and looked up the big bay toward Bell Rocks. She was worried and wondered what would come of the council.

CHAPTER 2

The Council

ONCE INSIDE his own house, Half Sky found he scarcely knew it, for cross-legged on the platform, where Crashing Thunder, Flying Cloud and White Goose slept, sat seven men. In the center was Chief Crashing Thunder, on his right Grandfather Footsteps of the Bear, next to him Sparrow Hawk, then Blackbird. On the chief's left sat Herb Gatherer, the doctor, next to him an old warrior, Sounding Rock, and then West Wind, the keeper of the drum. All were looked up to with great respect by the village. On the floor at the sides of the platform sat the other heads of households.

Half Sky stared at these familiar faces that seemed very unfamiliar now. They look solid, he said to himself, like the wooden images in Herb Gatherer's tepee. For a time no one spoke. Half Sky felt as though red-hot rays of light were trained on him from their eyes. Finally Crashing Thunder spoke.

"Half Sky, tell what you heard. All of us know Flying Cloud's dream about your hearing. Do not be afraid to speak."

Trying to keep the quaver out of his voice, Half Sky began by telling of his guessing game and how by chance his ear had rested on the ground. "I thought," he explained, "that it would be fun to see whether I could hear some of the little animals working beneath Birch Island. I had been wondering about Crow Tongue's stories of the Bad Matchi Manito and his imps, who deep down under the island plan mischief to us. Then I heard the drumming. I was scared, for I thought I was hearing the evil spirits. Little by little I made out the faint throbbing to be Iroquois war drums. I have done." He stood silent.

"How did you know they were Iroquois war drums, Half Sky?" demanded Blackbird.

He calls me Half Sky for the first time, the boy thought. Always before when he has joked with me he always has said Little Half Sky. For some reason the boy was frightened at the thought and could not keep the screech-owl tremolo out of his voice. He swallowed several times.

"I—I—Grandfather Footsteps of the Bear had told me about Iroquois war beats . . ." He stopped to steady his voice. No one on the platform showed that he noticed Half Sky's nervousness.

"Here, take this drum and beat out the rhythm as you heard it. Some of us have heard the Iroquois war chant." Blackbird reached behind him and brought out a skin drum and beater. He held them out to Half Sky, who made no move to take them, but looked at his father.

"Yes, Half Sky, make the drum say what you heard. Just what it said to you, mind." Crashing Thunder's voice was steady and encouraged his son.

Half Sky sat down cross-legged on the floor and inspected the drum to see whether the head was tight. He struck a few beats lightly. Bong! Bong! Bong! He nodded. His beater uplifted, he paused. He seemed to be listening to some far-off sound; then he began his drumming. It sounded a little choppy at first but soon settled itself into a pattern:

Boom, boom, boombo, boom! Dum, dum, dummity, dum!

Boom, boom, boombo, boom! Dum, dum, dummity, dum!

He was beating softly, but the sound filled the room. Blackbird flicked an eyelash at Grandfather Footsteps of the Bear. Suddenly from outside came Crow Tongue's voice.

"Iroquois war drum! War drum! War drum! What a dirty trick, to try to scare us. Maybe, though, it isn't a trick. If it's true—everybody pack up! Tear down the bark strips from the tepees. Let's go anywhere so it's away from the Iroquois. I know them. Didn't they almost get me? What ails all of you? Are you tied to logs? I tell you those Iroquois devils almost got me."

Blackbird muttered to Sparrow Hawk, "It's too bad they didn't." Aloud he said, "Crashing Thunder, tell Half Sky to go out and say to the mother of my wife, 'Stop talking and stay stopped unless you want your scalp dangling from some Iroquois belt.' "

"Go, Half Sky, take Blackbird's message to Crow Tongue."

Once outside, Half Sky gasped. The whole village was gathering up cooking pots, tearing off roofing mats and birch bark while Crow Tongue gabbled on. He walked up to her.

"Crow Tongue, Blackbird sends a message."

"Blackbird! Did you say Blackbird? That man! My daughter's husband, eh? Well, you tell him I send a message."

Half Sky didn't know whether he could outshout Crow Tongue but he tried. "He said to stop talking . . ."

"Stop talking!"

"Or your scalp will hang from an Iroquois belt."

Crow Tongue's mouth dropped open. She sank down on a log, her head in her hands. "Ooh, ooh, ooh," she moaned. The villagers stopped tearing their tepees apart and stood watching her.

Soon the men came out from Crashing Thunder's house and stood beside their chief, who said:

"We have taken thought and we have decided that, because of the keen ears given Half Sky by Flying Cloud's guardian helper, perhaps he has heard the war drums of our enemies, the Iroquois. I say perhaps. We must find out."

Just outside Crashing Thunder's house Sparrow Hawk now set up a red pole and from the top hung a scalp, the black hair blowing in the wind. In the open space near the pole stood West Wind with his red-blue-and-yellow drum. He started its steady song.

From all over the village, warriors, brilliant with red, yellow, and black paint, popped up as if by magic. Carrying bows and arrows and war clubs, they began to dance slowly around the red pole. Faster and faster they whirled until a warrior broke out of the circle, ran to the pole and hit it a resounding whack with his club. For a moment the drummers stopped. The song began again, and the dancers called "Whee! Whee! Whee!" and went through all the motions of hunting the trail, spying the enemy, jumping out and scalping him. "Whee! Whee! Whee!" they chanted again.

Chief Crashing Thunder, who led the dance, now stopped and held up his hand. He walked among the dancers and tapped ten men lightly on the shoulder. "Warriors," he said, "in making up a war party we ought by custom to fast for four days and then celebrate our war dance. We should then travel on a day's journey, make camp, and dance again. But this is not a war party. It is a finding-out party. We have little time to find out whether the Iroquois are near, and if so, how many, and what they intend to do.

"So let each of these ten I have picked go home and eat all he can hold. Let him take a pouch of parched corn powdered in the mortar and mixed with tree sugar. Let each man carry his bow and arrows, war club, and tomahawk, his dream bundle, three extra pairs of moccasins, a fur robe, and tobacco. Listen for my call to start."

Every man of the war party hustled back to his tepee. In almost no time at all, it seemed to Half Sky, who was getting the canoes ready, Crashing Thunder let out a great whoop. All the warriors, painted and armed, came running. They took their places in the canoes and, just as twilight was throwing long shadows of the birches over the water, in single file the slender craft glided in silence down the bay. Half Sky watched until they became little specks. Then he turned and went back to the round-domed house, now so empty.

Flying Cloud had a hot bean and venison stew, flavored deliciously with bear oil, and hot bread full of blueberries. Half Sky's appetite was gone. Only last night he had envied his father's ability to stow away great quantities of boiled fish and freshly baked bread. He could hear again his father's hearty "Oongh ondjita." Now only one night later Crashing Thunder with his warriors was slipping along in the shadows, looking for blood-thirsty Iroquois. The Iroquois might find him first. Half Sky bit off a piece of bread but could not swallow it, for his mouth felt full of dry bitter leaves. If only he had not heard the drums. A horrible thought came to him. Was it possible that he had only imagined he heard the Boom, boom, boom, of war drums?

"Little Half Sky," his mother said softly, "I think I know what you are thinking. Don't worry. Your ears are keen. Your protecting spirit will never lie to you. You heard aright, and you may have saved all of us from a surprise attack. Now come, eat. I put these blueberries in especially for you, because it's your favorite bread."

Half Sky picked up his bread, bit off a piece and tried to swallow. He pushed the bread away. "I'm sorry, Mother, but —but I can't forget it's Father's favorite bread, too."

The skin curtain at the doorway was raised, and Half Sky heard his mother say, "Nind ubimin, nind ubimin. Come in, Grandfather Footsteps of the Bear. Sit down. I made the stew and the blueberry bread that Half Sky is fond of, but he won't eat. Perhaps you can get him to taste his supper."

Footsteps of the Bear nodded. He loosened the wooden bowl and spoon that he carried tied to his belt and held out the bowl, sniffing the delicious steam from the cooking pot. Flying Cloud broke off a big chunk of the blueberry bread and passed him the bear oil.

"Oh-oh," said Grandfather Footsteps of the Bear, "so that's the way it is. Now, Half Sky, if you are going to do your father any good, you'll have to eat. Who do you think is going to bring in whitefish for your mother to smoke? Who but you?

And here you sit like your sister, little White Goose, and can't eat. Oh, oongh ondjita. My daughter, you are the best cook among the Ojibways. This really rolls round my heart." He took another helping of stew and more bread. "Such sweet bear oil."

Flying Cloud flushed with pleasure. Half Sky now managed to eat his bean and venison stew as well as a huge chunk of blueberry bread made tasty with bear oil. "I was hungrier than I thought," he admitted. Footsteps of the Bear flashed a look from his sparkling black eyes at Flying Cloud, who carefully stared at her bowl.

"I really didn't come to beg a dinner," he began. "I know Crashing Thunder had intended going to net whitefish for smoking. They should be running now at Whitefish Falls, and I wondered whether Half Sky wouldn't like to go with me. I am too old, Half Sky, and you are too young to go looking for Iroquois with your father, but what do you say we get up a party of old men and boys and bring home whitefish for winter? Our remaining warriors must stay home on guard."

Half Sky was so excited he got back more appetite and cleaned out the cooking pot and scraped up all the blueberry-bread crumbs. "Oh, I can hardly wait to go. Do you think I can get any fish? They say it is hard."

"You can learn. We'll need a lunch, Flying Cloud. What about starting at dawn? And another thing you'll have to be thinking about, Half Sky, is learning to make a canoe. We're short of canoes now because the war party needed them. We should have enough to get away from Birch Island in a hurry if need comes."

Finally, after Footsteps of the Bear had gone and Flying Cloud had banked the cooking fire with ashes, Half Sky lay down on his bearskin bed. He thought of whitefish flashing through frothy water and of canoes paddling silently through the dark night. He hoped the big water was not rough. It wouldn't be, though, because Father had bought from Herb Gatherer a charm for quiet water and a dark night. Half Sky listened but heard no waves crashing on Rocky Point, and the blackness was thick enough to cut. The charm was worth the venison it cost. Herb Gatherer has mighty medicine, he thought as he dropped asleep.

Flying Cloud's work had just begun. She pulled from under the platform the mohuk or birch-bark pail of parched corn. She carried it outside and put it in the wooden mortar; then with the pestle she pounded and pounded and sifted and sifted and pounded again. At last she had a small bark basket half full of finely pounded corn. With this she mixed maple sugar. She tasted it and said, "Crashing Thunder would say 'Oongh ondjita' at this." The maple sugar of last year, she was happy to say, was especially good, not bitter as Sparrow Hawk's, because he waited too long to tap the trees and so got buddy sap. She sighed as she laid out Crashing Thunder's nets.

She couldn't sleep because of what Footsteps of the Bear had said about leaving Birch Island, their home, very quickly "if need come." What did he fear? At last she fell asleep and dreamed. The big deer, the one she had dreamed about before Half Sky's birth, came to her in a cloud of smoke, it seemed. He walked up to her, licked her hand, and said,

"Crashing Thunder and the war party are running into danger. Tell Little Half Sky to fast and dream. If Crashing Thunder is saved, Half Sky must do it. Trust him. Send him to Herb Gatherer to buy a dream. Let him make peace with Big Face."

CHAPTER 3

Whitefish Falls

HALF SKY dreamed about catching a huge whitefish with his hands. Suddenly he thought he was being pulled into frothy rapids. Down, down, down he was dragged. Then someone shook him awake.

"Don't make a noise and wake up Flying Cloud," Grandfather Footsteps of the Bear said. "It's nearly dawn, and we want to get to Whitefish Falls at sunrise when the fish begin to run. We won't wait for breakfast. I have some corn meal and tree sugar if we get hungry."

Half Sky struggled to wake up. He was just tightening his breechcloth when he heard his mother say:

"Oh no, you don't go to Whitefish Falls and work all day on cold corn meal and tree sugar. You both need hot food. I have it already warm in the cooking pot. Besides, what would Crashing Thunder say!"

In a twinkling she had blown up the fire so it blazed about the cooking pot where the corn soup bubbled. She filled bowls for Footsteps of the Bear and Half Sky, then broke off huge chunks of hot bread with cooked beans in it. As Grandfather dipped his hot bread in the oil, he said, "Oongh ondjita, my daughter, this meal really makes a young man of me. There's nothing like nice sweet bear oil and hot bread."

After they had eaten, they collected Crashing Thunder's hand net and some woven bark bags to trail over the edge of the canoe if they caught more fish than the craft could hold. Grandfather and Half Sky hurried to the canoe landing where, besides Footsteps of the Bear's birch-bark canoe, nine others rocked gently up and down in the clear water. To Half Sky's surprise there stood Big Face with his great-uncle, Ten Feathers. Stepping lightly into the canoe Grandfather Footsteps of the Bear knelt at the stern and motioned Half Sky to the bow.

All the others took their places in their canoes and, with their short, stubby paddles poised in the air, awaited Footsteps of the Bear's word to go.

"Now," he said, and all together twenty paddles seemed just to touch the water at the same second. The canoes skimmed along the shore of Birch Island as softly as hunting owls. Like a great curling water snake, Half Sky thought, a ten-jointed giant water snake.

"Ha," Footsteps of the Bear chuckled, "as long as I get such feelings as this, Half Sky, I am willing to live on, even if I am old."

Until they reached Rocky Point he was silent, but when he glimpsed the smoke from the cooking fires of the village they were leaving behind, Footsteps of the Bear touched the medicine bundle around his neck and prayed, "Oh, Great Spirit, never let me sound the danger warning on Bell Rocks. May our Birch Island have peace for strings of lives."

An hour's steady paddling brought them to a portage. It was a very short one, so Half Sky hoisted the canoe over his head, carried it over a few feet of ground, and set it down in the clear green of North Channel water. Only six miles of easy paddling on a glassy surface brought the canoes to Whitefish Falls. With Grandfather Footsteps of the Bear first, since he was the oldest, the others lined up their canoes according to the age of each owner.

"Why, the river's alive with fish. Look at them—great white ones—just as I dreamed last night."

Footsteps of the Bear missed a paddle stroke. "Dream? What dream?" He touched his medicine bundle and looked at Half Sky anxiously.

"Oh, I dreamed I had a big, big fish in my hands. Somehow it took me down into the water, down and down and . . ."

"You must be very careful today, Half Sky. Your protecting spirit has given you a warning." Grandfather sat silent for several paddle strokes, then added, "Everyone is given a warning, but we are so stupid we seldom heed it."

"Look! Look, here is a whole school of the white ones. See that huge one! He must be . . ."

"Now don't get excited, Half Sky. That isn't the first whitefish in the world, nor the last. Besides, no good warrior ever shows surprise. Now you listen to me."

Footsteps of the Bear pointed toward white boiling water ahead. "The Falls. Those eddies around the rocks are places for getting whitefish. You kneel in the bow with your net held firmly in your hand. I will guide the canoe into the rapids, and you let your net down into the water right over the biggest bunch of fish you can. Give the landing net a quick turn and haul it up to the canoe. Don't worry if any fish get away; we'll get them later, perhaps. You just pull the net up to the canoe and lift it in.

"Your father used to stand up and net the fish as I did when

I was younger and as you will when you are older. Just keep your head, Little Half Sky. Scoop up all you can. You can rest after each netting while the other canoes try, and until our turn comes again to go over the rapids."

Skillfully Footsteps of the Bear steered the frail craft among the rocks, through the boiling rapids. Half Sky saw hundreds of fish. He let down his net. Fish filled it, but some swam right out again and away. He had all he could do to lift the net and had another tussle to bring it to the side of the canoe. By this time Footsteps of the Bear had piloted them into calm water and could help Half Sky bring in the net.

"Well done! Maybe your dream was good after all. You did much better than I did the first time I went out." Even though Footsteps of the Bear saw Half Sky was shaking, he pretended not to notice.

Back and forth over the boiling water went the Birch Island canoes all day long. Sometimes Half Sky got no fish at all; other times two or three. Never again did he net six. "Beginner's luck," Footsteps of the Bear grunted.

All the other fishermen except Big Face were tired. He hadn't netted as many fish as Half Sky and teased his uncle Ten Feathers to go over once more. Nearly all the party were busy arranging their fish to take home, and no one was watching Big Face and Ten Feathers except Half Sky and Footsteps of the Bear. Half Sky was secretly laughing because Big Face hadn't fared very well and was waiting to tease him about his bad luck.

Ten Feathers had carefully let the canoe down the rapids when Big Face began to yell, "It's the grandfather of all white-fish! I can get him, too. Half Sky hasn't one as big as this. I'll

Half Sky grabbed the unconscious boy by his long hair

bet it weighs more than . . ." In his excitement Big Face stood upright in the canoe and leaned over to bring up his prize. He lost his balance and fell into the seething water, net, fish and all.

For a second Half Sky couldn't believe it. Then he jumped in after Big Face, who had disappeared in the foam of the rapids. As Big Face came up, he grabbed Half Sky by the breechcloth and both went under the water. Up they came. Big Face was in a panic and pulled Half Sky under. Half Sky hit Big Face with his fist and then grabbed the unconscious boy by his long hair. With one arm he tried for the shore where Grandfather Footsteps of the Bear looked helplessly on.

It seemed to Half Sky that something had him by the legs pulling him toward the whirlpool. He felt he was weakening, and Big Face was as heavy as a bear. Suppose a water sprite had him. Who can fight an evil water spirit? Suddenly it didn't seem to matter.

Then he heard Footsteps of the Bear call, "The current, the current! Catch hold of this birch." The old chief had grabbed a slender birch and bent it out toward the water. "Catch hold of the birch!" he yelled again.

Half Sky reached for it. He couldn't touch it.

Ten Feathers stood on the bank crying, "Ula lu, ula lu, ula lu—alas, alas."

"Quit your lamenting! Grab hold of this birch and bend it down farther," Footsteps of the Bear ordered.

Ten Feathers threw his weight against the tree. "Ula lu, ula lu, ula lu," he began again, "it's going to break off."

But it didn't break. Slowly the two old men swung the tree nearer the struggling Half Sky. He grasped it. Little by little,

Footsteps of the Bear drew the two to shore where the other men, hearing the noise, had rushed to help. They pulled the boys up on the bank.

Ten Feathers began to work Big Face's arms up and down until the boy opened his eyes. Finally he sat up. He grinned at Half Sky, who was trying to get his breath.

"Hello, you dirty skunk—but, Half Sky, you're the best dirty skunk on Birch Island," he whispered.

Half Sky grinned and said between breaths, "Hello, you stinking fish. You aren't dead yet. But, Big Face, you're the best stinking fish on Birch Island."

Footsteps of the Bear took his bowl from his belt and mixed some powdered parched corn and tree sugar with a little water and made the boys eat it. In a few minutes they were ready to go home. They scorned the deerskin robes Ten Feathers had borrowed to wrap them in. "We're not babies," they told him.

Great content filled Half Sky. With a canoe load of fish, with Big Face a friend forever, he watched the paddles touch the water lightly and saw the birch trees on the mainland slip by. By the time they reached the portage Half Sky proudly raised the slight craft over his head and set it down in their own blue water—water that talked and laughed and crashed against Rocky Point of their own Birch Island.

As they neared the canoe landing, Footsteps of the Bear sounded the victory call, the sign of success in the hunt, "Yahoo, yahoo, yahoo." This told the village that the fishing party was coming in with plenty of fish. Everyone came running. Even before they landed, Half Sky could hear Crow Tongue.

"Well, here they are, but I thought they'd never make it. Old men and boys to get whitefish! The idea! I want my share, too. Haven't I thought good for you ever since you went out? Oh, Footsteps of the Bear, haven't you got a nice little fish for me, just right to broil? Big ones are coarse."

Half Sky laughed as did Footsteps of the Bear. It was good to hear Crow Tongue. She was part of Birch Island. It meant they were safely home.

"Oh, Half Sky and Big Face," Crow Tongue went on, "you'll have to give a first-fruits feast. You caught your first whitefish. Oh, I love first-fruits feasts. I'll go get my bowl and spoon. Flying Cloud makes the best blueberry bread on the island, and her planked whitefish—oh, la, la, la."

Half Sky watched Crow Tongue as she ran off. "Is it true? Do we give a first-fruits feast for whitefish?"

Footsteps of the Bear nodded. "Oh, yes. Luckily we have plenty. Besides our canoe full, I towed two bark bags full. You're doing pretty well as provider of a family."

Half Sky gave himself over to pleasant thoughts—hot bread, broiled fish, little cakes of dried sweet corn, stewed pumpkin. Tomorrow the feast of first fruits. Big Face and he were friends.

As they left the canoe, Half Sky could smell his mother's hot blueberry bread. She had bean soup, too, he found, and the delicious aroma of pumpkin flavored with maple sugar filled the air.

While Footsteps of the Bear and Half Sky were eating, Flying Cloud picked out a medium-sized whitefish, cleaned it, and after splitting it, pegged it onto a heavy board. Then she set it in front of the fire where it sizzled with delightful crackles. Several times she moved it back from the fire so it would cook slowly and not burn. "Crashing Thunder hates burned whitefish," she said to Footsteps of the Bear.

Just as she was ready to serve the fish and pumpkin, the skin curtain over the doorway was raised.

"Nind ubimin, nind ubimin. Oh, come in, Crow Tongue."

"Well, here I am just as I said. You can't keep Crow Tongue from a feast."

"The feast isn't until tomorrow," Footsteps of the Bear explained. "You must give Flying Cloud and Daylight Feather, Big Face's mother, time to cook the food before we eat it."

Flying Cloud laughed. "Give me your bowl, Crow Tongue. You are welcome to eat." She dished out the bubbling soup, gave Crow Tongue bread and bear oil. Then she divided the broiled whitefish and handed out the pumpkin.

"That's right," Flying Cloud said to Grandfather. "We do have to make the Feast of First Fruits, don't we?"

He nodded. "I think you'll be proud . . ."

Someone else raised the skin doorway curtain. "Nind ubimin. Nind ubimin," Flying Cloud called as Ten Feathers stepped in. He nibbled some pumpkin but said he had just eaten a big supper.

"I came, since Big Face's father is on the war party, to thank Half Sky for saving Big Face from the bad water spirit. It would have been terrible if his father had come home and found Big Face gone. I have done." He walked out of the lodge.

"My son, why didn't you tell me?" Flying Cloud asked. "What did he do, Footsteps of the Bear?"

"Half Sky is modest, as a young warrior should be. I'll tell you about it sometime, Flying Cloud. You will be proud."

Half Sky was partly pleased and partly embarrassed. He wiggled around and finally said he was going to bed.

"The best of it all," Footsteps of the Bear said, "is that Big Face and Half Sky are bound to be friends for life." Changing the subject, Grandfather said, "You will start smoking fish tomorrow?"

Flying Cloud for a moment was too proud to say a word. Finally she said, "Yes, tomorrow I start the smoking fires and make the Feast of First Fruits."

After Footsteps of the Bear left, Flying Cloud banked the cooking fire and put some dried beans to soak for tomorrow's breakfast. Then she, too, slept.

CHAPTER 4

The Feast of First Fruits

HALF SKY awoke at dawn. As he lay on his bearskin and listened to the *clink, clank* of the stones as his mother pushed them against the cooking pot, the *poom, poom, poom* of the pestle as it powdered the corn in the stone mortar, and the *klink, klink, klink* of the flint cutting through the dried fish, he thought how his father must miss those pleasant noises. He was sure the chief often thought of the tantalizing smell of the corn soup bubbling over the fire, of the fragrance of birch-wood smoke. Perhaps he missed even the raucous voice of Crow Tongue, who just now had come to borrow some bear oil—and, of course, to see whether Flying Cloud would invite her to breakfast. Half Sky knew that Crow Tongue was so snoopy she just had to know how many fish Flying Cloud was planning to smoke and how many she would cook for the feast.

He remembered what his father said once when someone complained that Crow Tongue was a nuisance. "Don't forget," he said, "Crow Tongue's husband was burned by the Iroquois. She herself escaped by ducking into a hollow tree. When the Iroquois looked in, they saw a bear and decided no squaw would dare hide there with a bear. I was on the war party that found her wandering in the forest, for strangely enough, the bear did not harm her. She has never been quite the same since. Now the Great Spirit guards her, and you and everyone else in the village must look at her as one on whom He has set his seal."

Half Sky was not surprised to hear his mother say, "Stay for breakfast, Crow Tongue. The soup is ready and the bread is nearly done. How would you like to make some of your good sweet corn cakes for the feast? I am too busy with all these fish to smoke and a First-Fruits Feast on my hands—and the chief away."

"Oh, my sister, thanks." Crow Tongue called Half Sky's mother "sister," because she belonged to the bear clan as his mother did. Of course, Flying Cloud's children were bears, too, as children always were considered in the mother's clan. Maybe that's why the bear didn't claw Crow Tongue, thought Half Sky. He knew she, too, was a bear.

Crashing Thunder belonged to the muskrats. The boy laughed when he thought of the chief belonging to the muskrats. Many brave warriors, however, were muskrats, for it was a big clan, even though it took its name from a small animal.

It was certainly no time for mooning around on a bearskin and Half Sky jumped up and rolled away his bed. Today his mother was using the outdoor cooking fire, for the weather was warm; besides she had to be outside to watch the fish smoking.

"Have you enough cooking pots?" Crow Tongue asked.

"I have two big ones, but I must borrow four more."

"I have two," Crow Tongue said. "I'll run and get them and stop on my way at Talking Water's and borrow hers."

"I don't believe you'll get them, because she is Big Face's

aunt and will lend hers to his mother for his feast. Besides, Talking Water is an otter and not so likely to lend to me as a bear."

"Well, I'll go to Herb Gatherer's. His wife is a bear."

Half Sky would have been glad to run these errands for his mother, but he had learned that men work with stone, making arrows and axheads. They also work in bone and make fishhooks; in shell and make wampum. The men make the canoes, the bowls everyone uses to eat from, and the spoons. They also build the framework of the houses and furnish most of the food the villagers eat. The men get the skins for clothing, and most important of all, Half Sky thought, the men must defend their families against all enemies whether men or animals. It was the men who had gone to find out whether the Iroquois were lurking around Birch Island.

Of course, he thought, a woman works hard, too, but she does different things. She plants and hoes the corn, the beans, the squash. She finds the wild potato, finds nut trees and gathers the nuts. All the berries—blueberries, raspberries, and strawberries—the woman picks and dries; she braids cedar and cornhusk mats as well. He must not forget how a woman makes the clothing and embroiders it with dyed porcupine quills, works for months on a turkey-feather shawl and makes every cooking pot.

Right now it was his job to worry about how to fill the skin bag with cooking oil, how to get venison to dry for the winter, how to finish the snowshoes his father had begun. He must also learn to make powerful bows and arrows, for his own were small. They did fairly well for grouse, turkeys, and rabbits, but they were not heavy enough for deer, moose, or bear. Just let him hear anyone say a man has the easy time in an Indian village.

He remembered, too, that every winter some villager on his way to or from his trapping ground broke through the ice of the bay. Sometimes he drowned, or froze to death. Often he lost his dogs and the whole catch of furs that he had planned to clothe his family in. There was the ever-present danger that an enemy raiding party, lying on their stomachs like snakes, would suddenly rise up and attack the village or in the middle of the night set the houses on fire. Oh, decidedly a man had the worse part. He didn't feel guilty about Crow Tongue's running around to borrow cooking pots.

After breakfast his mother said, "My son, can you put up the stakes for smoking?"

Even though he did not know much about it, Half Sky remembered what his father had done. He found the smoking stakes stored under the sleeping platform and set them up in a circle. His mother made a small fire of birch wood inside the circle of stakes, and on each splinter of wood she stuck a whitefish, head and tail on, but cleaned and scaled. She kept the fire smoldering and put windbreaks of birch bark about the circle to keep the smoke swirling about the fish.

Crow Tongue began, "Well, Little Half Sky, if you are going to give a feast tonight, you'd better hie yourself around and deliver the sticks. Just like a boy, thinks because he is going to be a man, he can sit around and watch women work."

"Oh, Half Sky, I forgot the invitations." Flying Cloud ran into the house and brought out a bark box full of sticks. "Now you go first of all to Herb Gatherer. Give him one of these invitations and ask him to come here as soon as he can. The other sticks give to anyone you want to come to your feast."

"Ha, ha." Crow Tongue laughed. "I'll eat all the goodies, because you can't eat anything at your own feast. Ha, ha, all the more for me."

Grandfather Footsteps of the Bear came up just then.

"I'll tell you how to eat at a feast tonight. I did it once."

"Why, Footsteps of the Bear, you know very well a boy can't eat at his own feast."

"I didn't say eat at his own feast. Why can't he, after greeting guests, drop in at his friend's feast and eat there? I did that once. Big Face can eat here."

Everyone laughed, especially Crow Tongue. Half Sky hurried off to Herb Gatherer's and to pass out his other invitations. On the way he met Big Face who was sauntering along with his invitations and looking glum.

"I don't think much of this idea of not eating at our own feast, do you, Half Sky?" he asked.

But when he heard Grandfather's plan, Big Face danced a little jig, and his scowl disappeared as he trotted off to deliver his sticks.

Half Sky found Herb Gatherer in his medicine house, looking over his deerskin packages of yarrow, skullcap, betony, dittany, all wrapped up in separate bundles and packed away in a white-ash splint box.

"I am glad to see you have lived another day," Half Sky began politely. "My mother, Flying Cloud, wonders whether you can come to see her as soon as you can. She'd like you to smoke, I think."

"I am not surprised Flying Cloud wants me," the medicine

man said slowly. He looked very solemn. "Tell her I will come right away."

Sobered, Half Sky gave out his sticks and hurried back. He found Herb Gatherer as good as his word, sitting inside talking to Flying Cloud and Footsteps of the Bear.

As the boy went in, he heard the medicine man say, "I'll need the divining tent."

"Come, Half Sky," Grandfather Footsteps of the Bear called, "you and I must put up the tent for Herb Gatherer. Your mother is sad about her husband and wants Herb Gatherer to use his magic.

"Do you want a sweat tent, too?" he asked of Herb Gatherer.

"No. I, too, have been sad and worried about Crashing Thunder and dreamed that Flying Cloud would send for me. Last night I went to the sweat tent by the water, and I have been fasting ever since."

From a white-ash splint basket hanging from a pole, Flying Cloud took a deerskin robe, a pouch of tobacco, and a pair of quilled moccasins. She laid these at Herb Gatherer's feet.

Footsteps of the Bear and Half Sky made a barrel-shaped tent about six feet tall. Grandfather peeled sixteen ashen poles for the framework and put a cedar pole in the center. This, too, he peeled but left a tuft of leaves at the top. From the highest part of the tent, Grandfather and Half Sky hung nine little copper bells with wooden tongues. The bottom part of the divining house was curtained off by a skin robe.

Herb Gatherer, his gourd rattle in his hand, entered the tent. The women stopped their work. Everyone watched and listened. For some time all was quiet, then suddenly the tent began to sway and shake as in a terrible windstorm. The bells jingled ceaselessly, and the cedar pole bent over, straightened up, and bent over again.

"The spirits have come," Half Sky whispered to Grandfather.

"Hush," Grandfather said. "You will scare them away, and then they won't talk to Herb Gatherer."

From inside the tent Half Sky heard, "O Eagle, my guardian spirit and help, tell me how it is with Crashing Thunder, if it please you. Here is tobacco for you."

Half Sky could see the white smoke drifting out from the hole in the top of the tent and knew Herb Gatherer was dropping pinches of tobacco on the little fire inside.

Someone answered in a soft, pleasant voice, "This is hard. I need help. I must call on my friend the turtle."

A shrill voice that must belong to the turtle said that now Herb Gatherer would find out what he wanted to know. The upper two-thirds of the tent shook wildly. More white smoke plumed out of the roof opening. Herb Gatherer shook his gourd rattle and sang over and over:

> "You promised to help me,
> You promised to let me see things far away.
> Now I need you.
> Tell me of Crashing Thunder.
> Keep your promise,
> Tell me of Crashing Thunder."

He shook his gourd rattle. The bells jingled. The tent shook until Half Sky thought it would fall apart. Then everything became quiet.

Toward twilight, Herb Gatherer stepped out looking worn and tired. Grandfather Footsteps of the Bear, Half Sky, and Flying Cloud moved toward him.

He looked at them blankly, but after a few minutes said, "The dream is smoky, cloudy. My helper, Eagle, has told me Crashing Thunder and his party are in danger. They need help. Too much smoke. Too much cloud. Eagle says:

> " 'Drum beats sent Crashing Thunder out.
> Drum beats can save Crashing Thunder.' "

Without another word, Herb Gatherer picked up the gifts Flying Cloud had set out for him and walked away. Half Sky looked at Footsteps of the Bear, who was fingering his medicine bundle and moving his lips. Flying Cloud had drawn her robe over her head and sat down near the cooking fire.

The words of Herb Gatherer rang again and again through Half Sky's mind:

> "Drum beats sent Crashing Thunder out
> Drum beats can save Crashing Thunder."

What could it mean? He wanted to go into the forest where he could be alone. He turned and ran. All he could think of was that he was the one who had sent his father into danger.

"You don't act like a boy who is going to celebrate a First-Fruits Feast tonight," someone called as he rushed along. He did not even turn his head. He felt as though a heavy stone sat on his chest.

When he was away from everyone, he sat down and thought. "Go to see Herb Gatherer. Go to see Herb Gatherer," someone seemed to tell him.

"All right. I'll go right now," he said. He took off his green-bead earrings, and his eyes filled with tears, for his father had brought these back from the shores of the Big Lake to the North. It seemed as though he could not part with this last gift from his father. Perhaps I can do something for Father, he thought as he walked to Herb Gatherer's tepee.

Even before he could raise the doorway curtain, Herb Gatherer called, "Nind ubimin, nind ubimin, Half Sky."

Forgetting the ceremonial questions he should have asked, Half Sky held out his green earrings and said, "My father—can you . . .?"

"I don't want these, Half Sky. You keep them. I know how you prize them. I was with your father when he got them. Your mother has already paid me. Besides, it was a poor dream I gave her. I, too, am worried about your father."

"No, I won't take them back. Use them for tobacco to burn for your helper." Half Sky pressed the earrings into Herb Gatherer's hand. "I feel I sent him into danger with my silly listening to drum beats. You are a magic worker. Can't you help?"

"I wish I could, but I repeated just what the spirits told me. I myself can't make anything out of it. Almost a riddle:

"'Drum beats sent Crashing Thunder out,
Drum beats can save Crashing Thunder.'"

Herb Gatherer dropped twelve pinches of tobacco on the fire. He sat silent for a long time. At last he turned to Half Sky. "I can give you a bit of help. I think the spirit liked your giving him the green earrings."

"What do you think I can do?"

Herb Gatherer puffed on his pipe and sprinkled twelve more pinches of tobacco on the fire. When the white smoke had drifted through the tent hole, he said, "I'd go to Rocky Point and sit there until the spirit of Birch Island Water tells what to do."

Even though Half Sky was disappointed at the vagueness of the advice, he thanked Herb Gatherer. "Thank the spirit, too, and pray that I may understand what the water says," he told the medicine man.

"Oh, Half Sky," Herb Gatherer called as the boy started to go. "Be sure to go to your feast tonight. The spirits will feel slighted if you don't, and you may lose their help. I think you are going to find out what that drum-beat riddle means."

Half Sky nodded and ran toward home. Footsteps of the Bear was talking to Flying Cloud, and he knew somehow they had been speaking of him, because their eyes brightened when he came.

"Don't worry any more, Mother," he said. "I have been to see Herb Gatherer, and I know how I can find out how to save Father."

"Trust the Good Manito, my son," Footsteps of the Bear said. "Give thanks tonight and honor the Great Spirit."

The guests began to arrive and the talk was of whitefish and hunting. Some played sticks; some the moccasin game. Soon the women served the savory corn cakes and the broiled fish. Half Sky ate none but urged everyone else to enjoy himself.

He did as Herb Gatherer advised and stayed at the feast, but he did not have the heart to go to Big Face's feast even though Big Face came to his house and ate everything Flying Cloud offered. He paid particular attention when Grandfather Foot-steps of the Bear thanked the Great Spirit for the plentiful whitefish. Herb Gatherer also prayed for prosperity and long life for Half Sky. As the last cooking pot was emptied, the feast ended, and, since everyone brought his own bowl and spoons, there were no dishes to wash.

Flying Cloud sighed. "Your feast was a great success, Half Sky. I think the Good Manito will tell us what we can do to help your father." She banked the fire and took one last look at the fish she was smoking.

Within a few minutes Half Sky's mother and little sister were asleep, but he lay on his bearskin bed and thought about,

> Drums sent Crashing Thunder out
> Drums can save Crashing Thunder.

Would tomorrow give him an answer? Finally he went to sleep.

CHAPTER 5

Rolling Eyes, the Fire Woman

HALF SKY knew what he had to do. "Drums shall save him, drums shall save him," beat a pattern in his mind so when his mother thrust a bowl of corn soup toward him and asked what else he wanted, he said, "Drums shall save him."

Flying Cloud dropped the bowl; the soup hissed as it splattered on the cooking fire. Quickly she pulled the bowl from the fire before it could burn and, after filling it again, handed it to Half Sky, who stared at her. He ate his breakfast to the throbbing rhythm of "Drums shall save him, drums shall save him."

All sorts of ideas whirled around in his head. Should he talk to his mother about his plans? Or did she have enough to worry about? He had never known his mother to show her feelings by dropping a bowl of good soup. He looked up. Where had she gone?

He went outside. White Goose with her doll was playing with two other little girls. "Where is our mother?" Half Sky asked.

"She's sitting down by the rocks."

Swiftly Half Sky walked to the rocky ledge by the water. There sat his mother with her robe pulled over her head.

"Mother," he said softly, "Mother, what is the matter?"

She did not answer. He gently lifted the robe from her face. She was crying. He had never before seen her cry about anything.

"Oh, Mother, what has happened? Tell me what I can do."

Flying Cloud shook her head. She smiled sadly and walked back to the cabin.

Half Sky sat down on the rock ledge and watched the white horses of the bay come charging in. "Oh, You who have this island in Your keeping, make these waves tell me what to do," he prayed.

"Drums shall save him. Drums shall save him," the water said.

Half Sky jumped up, ran to the cabin, and from the birchbark box trimmed with porcupine quills took his dearest treasure, a string of amethyst beads. As he held them up, the sun brought out the lovely shades of purple and lilac. He looked at them once more and then closed his hand over them and walked off rapidly. He stopped at Big Face's tepee. "Big Face here?" he asked.

"No. He's mooning around by the ledge somewhere. I don't know what ails him. You go and see what you can do, Half Sky. I declare, I don't know what's got into him," Big Face's mother said.

On the rocky shore, Half Sky found his friend staring at the water. Half Sky was scrambling down a steep, rocky path when Big Face turned and said, "Drums can save him."

Half Sky almost lost his footing on the mossy rock, and suddenly he knew why his mother had dropped the soup bowl. She, Big Face, and he himself had been given the same dream.

"Yes, Big Face, I had that dream, too."

"That's what the water talks about, too, isn't it?"

The boys looked at each other. Finally Half Sky stood up. "Come, it's time we go to Herb Gatherer. He will tell us what to do."

"But I haven't anything to pay him with," objected Big Face.

"What I have is enough for both. See!" Half Sky opened his fist. Big Face stared at the lovely amethyst necklace.

"But, Half Sky, you can't give that away. Your father brought it all the way from I don't know where."

"I'm not giving it away. I'm buying advice to save my father. Come, we waste time."

Not a word did either boy say as they hurried along to Herb Gatherer's tepee. They hesitated before raising the skin curtain in the doorway.

"Nind ubimin. Nind ubimin. Come in," Herb Gatherer called.

The boys entered and found him sitting cross-legged before the fire, with his stone pipe in his mouth. His ceremonial pipe, Half Sky thought.

"Sit," Herb Gatherer ordered. He did not look at the boys. No one said anything for a time. Herb Gatherer took his pipe from his mouth, knocked out the ashes from the bowl, and put it away in a deerskin bag. He then sprinkled twelve pinches of tobacco upon the fire and prayed to his manito. At last he looked at Half Sky and Big Face.

"So," he said, "you, too, had the dream that drums can save him."

Half Sky swallowed once or twice. Big Face looked startled. They could only nod.

After a bit Half Sky asked, "Can you lend me a pipeful of tobacco?"

Herb Gatherer silently handed over the tobacco pouch and Half Sky slipped in the precious amethyst beads.

"I'll have to see whether I have a pipeful left," the medicine man began as he took the pouch and pulled out the beads. He held them up in the sun where they twinkled and shone like a rainbow. He gasped at their beauty.

"You love your father very much," he commented. "Now let's hear your trouble, but I won't take them." He passed them back.

When Half Sky had told him of his own dream, of Flying Cloud's dropping the bowl of soup when he said, "Drums can save him," of her crying alone on the rocks, of Big Face's having the very same dream, Herb Gatherer nodded and sat thinking. He put twelve more pinches of tobacco on the fire and prayed again to the manito. At last he turned to the boys.

"The manito says we must get Rolling Eyes, the Fire Woman. She lives all alone on a little island down the bay. She will trace Crashing Thunder by her fire magic."

"Do you think she will do it?" Half Sky asked.

"Do it? Of course. She already knows about it. The manito has told her. She will be ready when I go for her."

"Can't we go?"

"No. No one but a midewiwin one can go to her island. I'll take her your beads.

"Be back here at twilight," Herb Gatherer continued. "I'll have Rolling Eyes. Also, the manito wants Footsteps of the Bear. No one else. Now go."

"I'm scared," Big Face told Half Sky. "Something must be bad to have Herb Gatherer get Rolling Eyes. She won't come, for my father said she would never leave her island and would not let anyone land there. She has bad medicine too, as well as good. She has hunting charms and sells good winds. They say, too, she flies all over in the shape of an owl. I am frightened!"

Neither Half Sky nor Big Face wanted to talk to anyone, so they walked along the rocky ledge. They weren't even hungry. At twilight they walked up to Herb Gatherer's tepee and were not surprised to see Footsteps of the Bear enter. Timorously the boys raised the skin doorway flap, but they almost rushed away, for sitting by the fire was the strangest squaw they had ever seen. Wrapped in a doeskin robe decorated with colored porcupine quills in strange figures, her black hair cut short like a warrior's, with great earrings of green beads that pulled her ears down almost to her shoulders, she looked at Herb Gatherer, who nodded.

"Rolling Eyes, this one is Half Sky, Crashing Thunder's son, the one who sent the purple beads. That one is Big Face, Sparrow Hawk's son."

She beckoned, and they walked over to her. Her black eyes seemed to look through them. Finally she waved them back.

"Ho," she said. "They are honest. Let's get to work. I want to get back home.

"Since I have told the winds to be quiet for a time, we will go outside," Rolling Eyes told Herb Gatherer.

On the level ground in front of the tepee, she sprinkled fine wood ashes an inch deep. On this she placed bundles of sticks in the form of tepees. "Each bundle," she said, "is an Ojibway village. Here," she pointed to a large one, "is Birch Island, and here is Iroquois Island."

Grandfather Footsteps of the Bear examined the map for some time. "Good," he said and nodded his head. "I could find my way by that."

Rolling Eyes stood looking at her map. Suddenly she began to shake, to roll her big eyes, to mutter strange words. "Ho, ho, ho, ho," she repeated over and over. She clapped her hands, twisted about and almost stood on her head.

To Half Sky's great wonder he saw ten fiery sparks jump from the Birch Island bundle. They skipped and hopped along in the dust and made funny little tracks as birds do in the snow. At another bundle of sticks they disappeared, then came jumping out, eleven sparks now. Very slowly they crept toward Iroquois Island. When they were almost there a smoke covered them and swirled about. When the smoke went away, there was not a sign of a spark.

Rolling Eyes began to flail the air with her arms and kick her feet in the ashes. She snapped her fingers and became quiet. Immediately the wind began to blow, and all at once the ashes whirled about high overhead. Not a trace remained on the ground.

Half Sky and Big Face rubbed their eyes. Grandfather Footsteps of the Bear was breathing fast. Rolling Eyes closed her eyes and sank down on the ground. When her breathing was quieter, she looked at Herb Gatherer. For a long time she sat motionless with folded arms. Finally she chewed up a red-hot ember from the fire, spat it out, and spoke.

"The fire has told me all. Crashing Thunder and his party set out from Birch Island with ten warriors. They went to the village on the Island of the Great Spirit. Here, one warrior joined them. Next they went to Iroquois Island where they were captured and are in great danger. The only good thing is that the Iroquois warriors are all young and untried. They came to spy on the Ojibway and find out what they could so that a big war party could come and wipe you out. They are angry because Crashing Thunder will not tell how he knew they were near. I think they want to burn all the Ojibways. No good.

"I will send feathers—so . . ." She reached into her pouch and took out a handful of feather-down. She threw it up in the air. "Go," she ordered, "go and jump into the young warriors' heads so they will be foolish. Go."

A high roaring wind took the feather-down. Half Sky and Big Face were scared, but Herb Gatherer asked, "Is there a chance of rescue?"

"Yes," Rolling Eyes answered. "By drums they were led out; drums shall set them free. Not by a war party. By trickery, yes. May your manito tell you what trick to use. I have done."

She arose, stalked to her canoe and soon was skimming back to her island. Grandfather Footsteps of the Bear went into the forest to pray to his manito. Herb Gatherer sat staring at the cooking fire. Half Sky and Big Face walked together toward the rocky point where the water talked loudest.

Half Sky called, "O spirits of the blue water that guard our Birch Island, I beg you to talk to me. Tell me how I can set free Crashing Thunder and the other brave Ojibways. You waters know. You have been here for strings and strings of lives. You love Birch Island. You have wisdom. Speak, I pray you. We listen."

The boy sat quiet. Darkness came. The moon made a bright path over the water that began to mumble, then to talk louder and louder. Suddenly it stopped. Everything was so still Half Sky could hear a porcupine gnawing in a cedar tree.

"I have it. I have it," Half Sky called to Big Face. "Let's go to Grandfather Footsteps of the Bear."

They hurried to Grandfather's tepee, but he was not there. Away they ran to Herb Gatherer's. As they touched the skin door, they heard, "Nind ubimin. Nind ubimin. Come in, Half Sky and Big Face. We are waiting for you."

Half Sky spoke breathlessly. "Herb Gatherer and Grandfather Footsteps of the Bear, the water has spoken. I know the trick. Let Big Face and me go to Iroquois Island. We will take drums. We will beat out the Ojibway Victory Song. Grandfather Footsteps of the Bear can sound the alarm on Bell Rocks. The Iroquois will think a big Ojibway war party is landing. Very big because they dare beat the drums. Since the Iroquois are few and Rolling Eyes has made them feather-brained, they will run. They are not Ojibways. They will go. 'Drums sent them out. Drums shall rescue them.' The talking waters have told me so. I have done."

Footsteps of the Bear looked at Herb Gatherer. Both nodded. "It is so. We will try it," they told Half Sky and Big Face.

CHAPTER 6

Drums Shall Set Him Free

FOOTSTEPS OF THE BEAR must have talked with Flying Cloud, for when Half Sky entered the cabin, his mother put her hand on his shoulder and handed him a drum. "My father's," she said. "It has beat out the Ojibway Victory Song for defeated Iroquois. May the Good Manito permit it to sound again—and if possible bring home your father."

She turned abruptly. Half Sky didn't know what to say. He took the drum, stood for a moment or two looking at the cabin, at his mother, at White Goose. Then he turned and walked away.

He met Big Face at Footsteps of the Bear's. Grandfather had been making a drum for Big Face. The old man sat outside his tepee with the drum in his hands.

"Hah," he said, "so Flying Cloud has given you her father's drum. It is good medicine, better medicine than mine. Let it guide you. Here is what I made for you, Big Face." He held out the skin-covered drum.

"When I hear the Victory Song come over the water, I will sound the alarm on Bell Rocks," said Footsteps of the Bear. "I have my father's war club that his father had. It is one of our treasures, and it alone can make the Bell Rocks ring. I will be there and the Rocks will ring. And may the spirits of our brave warriors who died fighting the Iroquois go with you and help you. I have done." He stood up, looked over the tumbling blue water toward Bell Rocks, then went inside his tepee and let the skin curtain down.

Outside, Half Sky and Big Face looked at each other. "Well," Big Face said, "it seems to be our job from now on."

Half Sky nodded. He looked toward Bell Rocks and listened to the voice of the water as it rolled along with white frothy crests.

Big Face pointed to the canoe landing where Herb Gatherer was standing. They turned and hurried to him. A trim birch-bark craft was ready and, tied to it by a strong spruce-root rope, six canoes bobbed up and down in the Birch Island water.

"Like as not," Herb Gatherer observed, "those Iroquois dogs have destroyed Crashing Thunder's canoes to make sure his party can't escape. If you rescue our warriors they will need something to get back in. Hurry, you don't have much time!"

Without another word, Half Sky knelt in the bow because he was a bit stronger than Big Face, who took his place in the stern. Softly they paddled out from the little bay.

"All right, your towed canoes are riding fine," Herb Gatherer called. "May I soon hear Crashing Thunder's voice raised in the hailing call and the Ojibway Victory Song for Iroquois prisoners."

Half Sky and Big Face found the work hard with the string of canoes trailing along, but the Indian craft rode the water well. The boys kept close to the shore so they could take advantage of the shadows and the calmer water. Just as the moon was making a silver path over the bay, the boys neared Iroquois Island. They stopped paddling and sat motionless in the dark.

"Too still," Half Sky said. "Big Face, I'm—afraid."

Somewhere a loon called. "Ah-o-o. Ah-o-o-o." The echo across the bay took it up. "O-o-o-o." Now the great horned owl screamed, "Whoo-who-o. Wh-o-o."

Another sound came—not a friendly loon or the great horned one—a faint crackling as though someone stepped on dry twigs. Half Sky bent forward and listened. Nearer and nearer came whoever was making the noise. Then Half Sky heard someone talking. Two, he thought, and both Iroquois. He did not understand what they said, but he listened for a familiar word. It came—"Crashing Thunder." When Half Sky heard his father's name, he gripped the paddle until his hand was numb.

All at once he heard someone say in the Ojibway tongue, "Soon we will see whether you Ojibways are warriors or squaws. When you feel the fire, you will show us. We will laugh at you."

Half Sky heard his father's deep voice. "Hah. We do not fear half-grown boys like you. Are the Iroquois so weak they send boys out to do warriors' work? Go home and get on your cradle boards. Tell your warriors we are insulted by striplings like you."

"Well, striplings can burn you. You will see."

Half Sky shuddered. Truly, Rolling Eyes and Herb Gatherer were right. There was no time to lose.

"We striplings despise you squaw Ojibways so much we haven't even tied you," a young piping voice taunted.

*The forest and rocks resounded with the Victory Song
of the Ojibways*

Half Sky prayed to the spirit of the drum that he and Big Face might beat out their Victory Song as no one else had ever sounded it. "Now," he whispered as he raised his drum beater. "One—two—three. Now!" All at once the forest and rocks resounded with the great Victory Song of the Ojibways. Boom, boom, boom, boomity, boomity, boom. Almost immediately the ringing tones of Bell Rocks came over the water. Clang, clang, ding, dong, clang.

"They're here. They've come. My people! Hear the Victory Song. Hear the great throat of our guardian, the Bell Rocks," Half Sky heard his father call. "They sound the alarm. Our Ojibways are coming."

"It may be a trick," one of the Iroquois said.

"Trick or no trick, I don't intend to be dragged back a prisoner. I don't want to land in any Ojibway village," another said. "We aren't any match for them. I'm going while I can."

"And I, and I, and I," Half Sky heard, as canoes grated on pebbles. Paddles splashed in the water as the Iroquois pushed off.

"Hah!" grunted Half Sky. "They aren't even good paddlers, splashing water like a young girl. Hah."

A scream filled the night. "Wait! Wait for me," someone begged. "Don't go away and leave me."

But no canoe put back.

Half Sky and Big Face watched the seven canoes driven forward over the water by the terrified Iroquois. The boys kept up their drumming while the whole bay echoed to the alarm of Bell Rocks.

When the boys could no longer see the Iroquois canoes, they stopped their drumming. They paddled to the pebbly beach.

"Father, Father!" Half Sky called.

"Half Sky!" someone answered. "I am Blackbird." He came forward into the moonlight and stared at the two boys. Finally he said, "But where are the others? The other warriors?"

"Others? There aren't any others. We're alone. We didn't have time to get anybody else. Rolling Eyes said the Iroquois were getting ready to burn you."

"Hah, hah," Blackbird grunted, and a grin spread over his face. "Alone. Hah! Crashing Thunder will forget his hurt when he hears this."

"His hurt?" Half Sky's eyes opened wider. He jumped out of the canoe and ran up to Blackbird.

"Here, this way," the warrior beckoned, and began to go up a rocky path until he reached a big flat rock. Half Sky saw his father leaning against a cedar tree.

"Father," he asked, "where are you hurt?"

"Hah. Only a scratch. Boys that ought to be carried about on cradle boards tried to hurt Crashing Thunder." He tried to get up but sank back. "I want Blackbird to pull this little flint splinter out of my shoulder, but he won't. I'd do it myself if I could get a good hold on it. Hah."

"We don't want to pull that axhead out until Herb Gatherer is around to take care of it," Blackbird explained. "And Herb Gatherer was wise when he thought the Iroquois might destroy our canoes. They broke them all to pieces. It takes a long time to make good canoes like ours. But we have two prisoners. I see someone has tied them up with the same thongs the Iroquois planned to use to bind us to the stakes. Hah! The cowardly dogs ran off and left these two."

Quickly Blackbird and Half Sky got Crashing Thunder into a canoe. When the chief protested that he was no baby, Half Sky said, "Herb Gatherer and Grandfather Footsteps of the Bear are waiting to hear you lead us in the hailing call and the death yell. Save your strength so you do not disappoint them."

"Hah," said Crashing Thunder, but he made no more objections. The water in the big bay was talking now, and the wind was against them so paddling was hard. After three hours, however, they could see Birch Island ahead. As they rounded the point, Crashing Thunder gave the hailing call and death yells, twice, telling everyone he had two prisoners and that he and his party were safe.

At the hailing call, everybody rushed either to the chief's cabin or to the canoe landing, where Crashing Thunder again gave the hailing call and the two death yells. The wounded chief insisted on walking to his cabin where Herb Gatherer was waiting. But when he reached his home, he sank down quietly onto a bearskin mat in front of the house. "Must see the Iroquois dogs run the gantlet," he explained.

Everyone in the village had picked up some stones or a club, and when one of the naked Iroquois prisoners came running down the path, a great yell went up. Everyone tried to pelt him with stones or hit him with a stick. He managed to reach Crashing Thunder's house and stood gasping and bleeding.

No one except a guard paid any attention to him, for the other prisoner came stumbling down the path. Someone had hit him hard as he ran, for he scarcely knew what he was doing. He collapsed in a heap almost at Crashing Thunder's feet. Guards hauled away the bruised and bleeding Iroquois.

Everyone was waiting to see what Herb Gatherer could do for Crashing Thunder. The medicine man looked carefully to see where the flint axhead had entered. He then opened a deerskin bag and took out a few leaves. He chewed these up and made four pills which he told Crashing Thunder to swallow. In a few minutes the chief's eyes regained something of their sparkle, and he ordered Herb Gatherer to yank out that Iroquois sliver.

The medicine man asked Flying Cloud to get warm water. He then opened his medicine bag and selected another pouch. From this he took some reddish leaves and crushed them to powder in his palms. As soon as the water was warm, he dropped several pinches of the powdered leaves into it. He grasped the axhead and pulled it from Crashing Thunder's shoulder. The chief did not wince or move. Quickly Herb Gatherer poured the warm liquid into the wound.

From other green leaves he made a poultice and laid it over the deep wound. Herb Gatherer began to hum softly as he massaged the hurt shoulder. On and on he sang, sometimes stopping to shake his rattle. At last the chief slept, but Herb Gatherer only sang louder and rattled his gourd. No one but Crashing Thunder was allowed to sleep, and Half Sky and Big Face had to be kept awake by Blackbird. "Sleep now is bad medicine for you," Herb Gatherer pointed out. "The spirits will not like it and the chief will be worse."

When Crashing Thunder woke up, he seemed better, but Herb Gatherer took off the poultice and examined the shoulder. He shook his head. "There is something inside there that is making trouble," he said.

Flying Cloud brought out two deerskins and a box of green stones. "Smoke for Crashing Thunder," she said and handed Herb Gatherer a tobacco pouch. He smoked a few puffs then put away his stone pipe and asked Flying Cloud for water "to put in a hollow bone." He took the leg of a small bird from his medicine bag, and holding the bone high over his head in his left hand, he took his rattle in his right hand. Rattle, rattle, rattle it went, again and again, as he beat his back, his breast, his arms with the gourd.

Then he began to talk, at first mumblings that became yells, then his voice dropped to a whisper. Only a word or two could Half Sky understand, but he knew the medicine man was calling on all good spirits to help Crashing Thunder.

"Oh, Thunderbird that sees everything in everyone's heart, everything in the ground, and everything in the water, help Crashing Thunder. Everyone is afraid of you. Help Crashing Thunder."

He put the little bone in his mouth and swallowed it, while he shook his gourd. Rattle, rattle, rattle filled the room.

"Oh, little bone in my throat," he prayed, "help Crashing Thunder. Oh, you say you will if I let you out? Well, then, out you come."

With a terrific shaking of the rattle, Herb Gatherer brought up the bone from his throat and spit it out onto his hand. He blew on it. To Half Sky's surprise it whistled like a woodpecker. Tootle-de-tootle-de-tootle.

Herb Gatherer laid the bone next to the ax wound and, to everyone's astonishment, he sucked into a bowl dozens of little yellow worms with red heads. They wiggled and twisted like eels.

"Burn these worms," he told Half Sky, "or they will run back into the wound and kill Crashing Thunder." Half Sky burned them in the cooking fire. The smoke was dense and the smell bad.

Herb Gatherer made a fresh poultice of crushed herbs and laid it on the wound. Then he began to shake his rattle and call on Thunderbird again. At first Crashing Thunder was restless and feverish, but soon he slept. When he woke up hours later, his shoulder was lame, but he got up and walked about as usual. At sundown he was able to sit at the council.

Flying Cloud was hustling about cooking fish with dried sweet corn and squash. "You don't look as though you have had anything to eat at all," she said to her husband. "Those Iroquois starved you."

He laughed. "It's worth fasting to come home to your cooking."

Crow Tongue came in just then. "Oh," she cackled, "I'm just in time for that fish soup. I have my bowl with me, too. Aren't you proud of Half Sky? When does he fast on Dreamer's Rock? What I really came to ask about is this: I'm putting in my bid for one of those young Iroquois bucks as a husband.

Now, that's no more than fair because the Iroquois killed mine. I tell you, Chief, it's no fun to live alone and watch the bear oil shrink every day and see no great hunks of venison, no juicy beaver haunches in the tepee. I think it's my due and . . ."

"My husband has been sick," Flying Cloud said gently. "Don't talk to him now."

"Well, what if he has been sick? He's better now. I must say people aren't very grateful. I asked that good-looking Iroquois whether he wouldn't rather be my husband than be burned. And what do you think he said?"

"What did he say?" Crashing Thunder was amused.

"He just looked at me as impolite as you please and turned his head."

Crashing Thunder looked at Flying Cloud, who had to go outside to keep from laughing.

"Well, what do you want me to do, Crow Tongue?"

"How many times do I have to tell you? Give me the good-looking one as a husband."

"Well, I'll tell you what I'll do. I'll take that up with the council tonight. I promise you I'll do my best."

As soon as Crashing Thunder had rested, the council began. Footsteps of the Bear, Sparrow Hawk, and Blackbird were there along with Herb Gatherer, Sounding Rock and West Wind.

Each began, "Has Crow Tongue been after you?" Then a smile passed over their faces.

The warriors agreed to have a victory dance as soon as Crashing Thunder's shoulder was healed, and to send Rolling

Eyes a new birch-bark canoe, a haunch of venison, dried white-fish and a bearskin mat.

"I have had a dream telling us we should send Half Sky and Big Face to Dreamer's Rock," Blackbird said. All agreed.

"But what are we going to do about Crow Tongue?" Crashing Thunder asked.

Footsteps of the Bear took a puff on the pipe that was being passed around.

"Do you think we could give her the younger Iroquois as a slave and promise her the next older Iroquois we catch as a husband?"

"Your words are wise," Blackbird said. "And we ask you, Footsteps of the Bear, if everyone agrees, to tell her our decision." They all nodded.

Footsteps of the Bear looked anything but pleased and started to protest.

"It's the wish of the council," Crashing Thunder told him.

Blackbird spoke. "I think we should do something for Half Sky and Big Face. If Half Sky hadn't dreamed of Iroquois drums and if he and Big Face and Footsteps of the Bear hadn't used their wits, some of us wouldn't be here today. I think we should ask Herb Gatherer, who is also a singer, to make up a song for the dance that Half Sky and Big Face will give when they come from Dreamer's Rock."

The whole Council nodded agreement. "And mind you," cautioned Blackbird, "let's keep this a secret. Don't let Crow Tongue get hold of it."

When the council broke up, Grandfather Footsteps of the Bear stayed for a bit to talk to his son.

"That was a pretty bad trick, to ask you to tell Crow Tongue we will give her a slave, not a husband. I'm sorry for you," Crashing Thunder said.

"Hah. I've lived many moons, handled many Crow Tongues. You, my son, are safe. Hah." He raised the skin curtain and stepped out into the night.

CHAPTER 7

Rice Gathering

"THE RICE is ready on Vermilion River," Half Sky told Big Face one morning. "We'll all be going there soon."

"How do you know?"

"Chief Rest a Long While from the Island of the Great Spirit sent word. The women are getting out the rice bags and West Wind and Ten Feathers are out looking for a moose so we will have meat to take. The game around Vermilion River isn't good."

Just then the crier began announcing that tomorrow at sunrise the whole village would set out for Vermilion River to harvest the wild rice. Everyone began to scramble about. The men inspected the canoes and the bows and arrows. The women packed up dried corn, braided dried squash and selected some dried fish and venison. Everyone laughed and joked.

Rice gathering was fun. West Wind boasted he would harvest ten bags, and Blackbird was sure he could get even more. Cooking fires burned late, and White Goose and the other girls sewed woven bags with big uneven stitches. These bags were about sixteen and one-half inches long and had arms and legs. They looked like dolls without heads. The ends of the arms and legs were woven solid and at the neck was a drawstring. These odd-looking bags let air circulate and kept the rice from heating and moulding.

Other girls were weaving bags of cedar bark. Half Sky and Big Face stopped to look at these bags and were glad that weaving was women's work and they could not be asked to help.

"Half Sky, I have often wondered why White Goose and other girls hoe corn, weave bags and cook, and why we boys hunt, fish, and even go for wild rice," Big Face observed.

"Here comes Footsteps of the Bear," said Half Sky. "Let's ask him."

When they asked Grandfather why men should not do women's work, he said, "Because the Great Hare ordered it that way. Long, long ago my grandfather told me that a man was hunting when he found the footprints of a giant.

"Even though the man was somewhat scared, he followed the footprints and there just ahead towered the biggest tepee he had ever seen. Near it stood what he first thought to be tall pines, but which turned out to be the feet and legs of a giant. His head he could not see, for it was hidden away up in the clouds.

"The man was so scared he hid in some brambles, but the giant saw him and called, 'My child, why are you afraid? Take courage. I am the Great Hare. I caused you to be born from dead bodies of animals. Now I will give you a help-meet.'

"He gave the man a wife and said, 'Woman, you shall do the cooking for your husband, make his shoes, mittens, and dress from skins of animals. You shall weave, sew and make garden.'"

As Grandfather Footsteps of the Bear stopped his story and walked on, Half Sky said, "Well, the Great Hare divided the work pretty well after all, didn't he?"

Big Face nodded. "That reminds me. While we are gathering rice we should watch out for some especially good birch bark. You know we have to make our own canoes now."

Flying Cloud called from the cabin, "Here, you boys who want to do men's work. Come, Half Sky, look at the grease bag. It's empty, and so is the meat rack. While your father's shoulder is bad, you are the man of the house. I have some dried and braided squashes, enough corn meal until the harvest, and some dried whitefish. But I need bear oil. What is corn soup without nice sweet bear oil?"

"Well," said Big Face, "perhaps being a boy isn't such a great thing after all."

The boys walked in silence until Half Sky said, "I don't know how I am going to fill Mother's grease bag."

"I suppose we could get a bear," Big Face answered.

"Remember the time we saw a boy who had been clawed by a bear?" Half Sky looked solemn.

"Yes, I do remember. Perhaps we should stick to partridges and let your mother borrow bear oil," Big Face suggested.

Later, when Half Sky and Big Face were walking along the rocks, Half Sky said:

"I'm going out to look at my rabbit snares. Want to come?"

They trudged off together. Each had his bow and two arrows.

"Look!" Big Face warned. "Do you see what I do?"

There by the snare and trying to pull out the dead rabbit was a big bear. Half Sky was trembling so he could scarcely set the arrow. What are you, a coward? he asked himself. Didn't you beat the Ojibway Victory Song right under the noses of the Iroquois?

He let his arrow zing. It went into the bear somewhere, because the bear roared and came rushing toward Half Sky.

Big Face climbed a tree and went far out on a slender branch. "Shoot him again, Half Sky," he called.

Half Sky shot once more but couldn't see that it made any ifference to the bear. He just roared louder and kept crashing on.

"Climb the tree, climb the tree!" Big Face called.

In a panic, Half Sky followed the advice. He scrambled up and up and crept out onto a branch so tiny that he was sure it would never hold a bear.

Down below, the bear loped along, roaring as he came. Half Sky was terrified when the maddened animal began to climb the tree. How far could he come? Half Sky remembered his grandfather's saying, "A bear can outclimb, outswim and outrun any man." To Half Sky's horror, he found he had dropped his arrows when he started up the tree. Nearer and nearer came the bear. Now he stopped and was looking at the boy crouched on the limb. Half Sky was sure the bear was laughing.

Something whizzed by. From the next tree Big Face had shot his last arrow. It struck the bear in the side. Half Sky held his breath. For a few seconds, the bear seemed to freeze to the tree, then he moved a shaggy paw over his hurt, suddenly loosened his hold and slid down the tree. The boys watched the black furry body as it flailed about, and when it lay still, they cautiously crept down.

He let his arrow zing

Big Face tiptoed up to the huge animal. "Dead," he called. "How did I ever do it? I must have been guided by my manito. Come down, Half Sky."

Trembling and shaking, Half Sky finally reached the ground. "That's—that's wonderful, Big Face," he managed to say. "You saved me. I thought he was coming right out on that branch to get me. Then he laughed at me because I was afraid. Did you see him laugh, Big Face?" Half Sky shuddered. "And I was the one who was going to get a bear so easily— like that." He tried to snap his fingers, but they were too numb to move.

Now it was Big Face's turn to say, "Pooh, I was just lucky, that's all. Of course my manito helped me. Anyway we have some bear oil, but what are we going to do with such a big, fat bear? I'll have to go for help. You stand guard and I'll find someone to help carry our meat in."

Soon Half Sky heard voices. Grandfather Footsteps of the Bear, Ten Feathers, and Sparrow Hawk were returning with Big Face.

"Hah," Footsteps of the Bear called as he stepped out of the underbrush. "What a bear! Who killed it?"

"Big Face," Half Sky answered.

"Half Sky," Big Face contended. "He wounded him."

Grandfather laughed. "Well, there's enough for all of us. Flying Cloud won't have to borrow bear oil. Hah!"

As they came near the village, Footsteps of the Bear told Big Face and Half Sky to give the hailing yell and the long victory cry. When the villagers saw the enormous bear with his rolls of fat, they gabbled and cried, "Hah! Hah! Hah! Plenty bear oil."

Flying Cloud and Crashing Thunder rushed out with the others and stood astonished when Grandfather said Big Face and Half Sky had killed it. The chief listened to the story of how they had found the bear and of how it had almost got Half Sky. When both boys said they wanted to divide the meat, Crashing Thunder looked at Sparrow Hawk and said, "They will do."

Flying Cloud cut up the fat from her portion of the bear and boiled it; then she skimmed off the oil and filled her almost empty grease bag. She kept the heart for her husband and gave the breastbone to Big Face, but he insisted Crashing Thunder eat it because it would heal his shoulder. The meat was so delicious and fat that nearly everyone in the village had a juicy steak to broil over the coals or a tasty chunk to boil. Flying Cloud would have dried some but, since they were to leave in the morning, she had no time.

At sunrise the next morning nearly all the villagers started in canoes for the rice fields in the marshes of Vermilion River. Like a huge family picnic, everyone was carrying food. Also in the canoes were strips of birch bark to serve as a roof for a sort of camper's shelter. At an astonishing speed they sped along, and stout young warriors made the portages in double-quick time. By afternoon they had arrived at the rice fields, great stretches of marsh covered with wild rice. Slender stalks, heavy with ripened grain, swayed slightly in the wind. The women set up cooking pots and started to bake bread.

Half Sky noticed that this year someone had been there earlier and had bound the rice straw together in bunches so the canoes could go between the rows of rice stalks and easily bend them down over the canoe and strip them of their oat-like grain. The rows of rice stalks seemed endless, and the work grew tiresome, but Half Sky and Big Face remembered how good this wild rice tasted with their mothers' delicious broiled duck, and they went to work harder than ever.

When the canoe was full of rice, they dumped it into a hole that Grandfather Footsteps of the Bear had the Iroquois slave make. Then he walked on the rice until the hulls came off. The next day he spread it out so the sun could dry it, and when he was sure it was dry, he packed it into bark pails and woven cedar bags.

At night everyone visited from one cooking fire to another. They told riddles, swapped stories, and sent the children to bed afraid to breathe because of the tales of the Bird that Flies by Night, the one with huge round eyes, the pet of the Black Medicine Woman.

Half Sky and Big Face glanced fearfully around and hoped no witches would fly about that night. The witches might sit on their chests, Crow Tongue said, and slowly smother them to death. The only thing they could do was to kill the Bird with the great round eyes. The boys took their bows and arrows to bed with them.

Half Sky had shown so much interest in the witch story that Big Face decided to play a joke on him. When he thought Half Sky had gone to sleep, Big Face wiggled out of his bearskin and sneaked over to Half Sky's shelter. He crept up to his sleeping friend and put a piece of wood on his chest, then he began to moan, "Hoo, Hoo, Hoooo."

Half Sky jumped up so fast that he surprised Big Face who tried to back into a dark corner but stumbled and sat down on the banked cooking fire.

"Ouch—hiyi," he yelled and jumped up. Luckily the coals were well covered with ashes and the only damage was a hole burned in his new deerskin leggings. The worst of it was that the whole camp heard about the joke and for a long time called Big Face the Bird with Round Eyes.

After a time, the longest yarn was ended, the long drawn-out game of sticks came to an end, the hungriest warrior filled his stomach with one last bowl of bear stew, the last cooking fire was banked and the rice gatherers slept.

CHAPTER 8

Time To Go to Dreamer's Rock

AFTER TWO more days of rice gathering, they all got into their canoes and paddled back to Birch Island. Crashing Thunder's shoulder was almost well again, but he was ill at ease.

As soon as Half Sky had taken up his paddle, his father said, "I'm worried. I'm afraid the Iroquois will strike before we are ready for them. I think it's about time, Half Sky, you begin taking charcoal for breakfast."

Half Sky knew what his father meant: he should begin fasting so he could go to Dreamer's Rock. He nodded.

His father went on, "The leaves have turned, so there is no danger of your dreaming of the Green Man."

Well did Half Sky know about this Green Man, for two years earlier West Wind's son had gone to fast on Dreamer's Rock during the summer. The Green Man appeared to him and promised the boy he should live as long as the Green Man. Of course, this man in the dream was the spirit of the leaves and when the fall came, and the leaves fell, the boy died. Half Sky knew that it was unlucky to fast on Dreamer's Rock except in the spring and fall.

"I want you to find your manito before I go on the war-path. I worry about dying before you see your manito and celebrate your feast. I want to stand for one of you at the feast. It's a father's proudest day."

"But Grandfather Footsteps of the Bear could do it, if you weren't here, couldn't he?"

Crashing Thunder looked at Half Sky for a time as if wondering how much to say; then he whispered, "Your grandfather has had a dream that he will never use his snowshoes again. That's another reason I'd like you to go now to Dreamer's Rock."

"Oh, but Grandfather's dream could mean . . ."

Crashing Thunder answered, "You must remember your grandfather has lived many, many moons."

"Then I begin the fast today?" Half Sky looked solemn.

"Yes. When your mother offers you venison stew in one hand and charcoal in the other, take the charcoal. Fast one day in four; then two days in four; then three days. Finally you go to Dreamer's Rock with Big Face."

"Then Big Face will go also?"

"Yes, it is easier so. When two go together, one can encourage the other even though you are not together all the time."

No one said another word until Birch Island came into view. As they neared the canoe landing, Crashing Thunder stood up and called, "Stay where you are until Blackbird walks about to see whether anyone has been here while we were away. Blackbird has sharp eyes.

"Do you have your arrows ready?" he asked the boatload of warriors next in line. They nodded. "Watch Blackbird," he ordered. "Keep your eyes on him."

Almost motionless the little group of canoes wavered on

the glassy water while Blackbird noiselessly stepped onto the pebbly beach and softly walked toward the tepees of the village. He watched the ground, the forest beyond, and the birch trees near the chief's house. He stopped. They all saw why he froze. What looked like a huge man stood outlined for just a second against the trees, then disappeared behind Crow Tongue's tepee.

"Hah," whispered Half Sky, "Blackbird's trailing him."

Crashing Thunder raised his hand for silence. All the men sat with paddles upraised ready to send the canoes leaping away from the island if danger threatened. What if the Iroquois were hiding in tepees and behind trees waiting for the villagers to get out of the canoes? A great silence came over the group.

Crashing Thunder sat like one of the rocks on the headland. He watched for Blackbird. If he did not see him soon, he would give the signal for flight. Was it an ambush?

"Half Sky," he whispered, "use your keen ears. Do you hear anything at all?"

The boy closed his eyes and put his whole mind on sounds. He heard the water talking, but it did not warn him. The wind soughed aimlessly through the pines and birches and rattled the poplars.

"A stick breaks under a footstep," he whispered to his father. "Now another twig—now many branches crash. It sounds like a blundering animal." He listened again, then opened his eyes and laughed. "I think it's a bear."

Fearful and impatient to get away, the people strained their eyes and ears. Suddenly they heard Blackbird's hail call and the death cry. "Yahoo," he called.

"O-ho," Crashing Thunder answered.

The warriors from the second boat piled out and ran in the direction of the sounds. Everyone followed and saw behind Crow Tongue's tepee the biggest black bear they had ever seen. Blackbird had sent an arrow into its heart. All about the bear were strewn a grease bag, woven bark bag of dried blueberries, and a bark pail of honey—the honey nearly gone.

"Here's a nice mess, I do declare," Crow Tongue sputtered. "All my honey gone, my blueberries thrown around, and my tepee clawed to pieces. It's a wonder we didn't leave someone on guard here."

Someone laughed. "Now, Crow Tongue, that's what we gave you the Iroquois slave for. Let him clean up the mess and get more honey for you. Besides, you should have put your honey away where nothing could get it," a young warrior said.

"Of all the impudence," Crow Tongue began.

"Let's be grateful it's no worse," Crashing Thunder said.

"Well, I claim the bear," Crow Tongue clamored.

"I think the bear should be divided between you and Blackbird," said Crashing Thunder.

"Oh, all right, all right," returned Crow Tongue.

Tonight in honor of the rice harvest and in thankfulness for the enemy's having turned out to be only a bear, Flying Cloud decided to make a special bread for supper. She called White Goose to bring in twelve ears of sweet corn. Flying Cloud had brought live coals in a cooking pot from the camp at the rice fields and with a few pieces of thin birch skin she had a fire going to roast the corn. With deer jaws White Goose scraped off the kernels of corn to put in the bread.

Flying Cloud mixed this scraped sweet corn with dried meal and blueberries soaked over night. It smelled delicious as it began to bake before the fire.

In the cooking pot was boiling dried venison pounded to powder and mixed with parched hard corn and red kidney beans crushed together in the mortar. Half Sky wrinkled his nose in delight, then suddenly realized that tonight he must refuse food and take charcoal. He felt what Grandfather said was true: "For every power a young warrior gains, he loses a greater pleasure of youth."

He knew, too, how everyone would begin to act toward him. Before, when it had happened to someone else, he had thought it funny. But he must act grown-up now, so when his mother brought a big chunk of corn and blueberry bread in one hand and charcoal in the other, without any hesitation, Half Sky took the charcoal. To show his father and mother he had strength of will, Half Sky watched the family eat with what he hoped looked like indifference. Finally he wandered off.

As soon as he was out of sight of the house, he hurried to Big Face's tepee. Sure enough, there sat his friend watching a porcupine chew up cedar leaves.

"Hello," Big Face said. "I suppose you took charcoal to-night, too. That porky's having a meal, anyway."

"Yes. I suppose one of the older men had a dream about our going to Dreamer's Rock?" Half Sky asked.

"Yes. I don't hold it against him, but I had hoped he'd wait," Big Face answered. "I don't know about growing up. Sometimes I wish we could stay just as we are. Oh, well, I guess we might as well go now as any time."

Both boys watched the porcupine feast on the cedar leaves. "*He* doesn't have to fast, does he?" Big Face went on. "Your father is a great joker, isn't he?"

"Yes. But what makes you ask?"

"He kept his face so straight I didn't know whether he was joking or not. He didn't say anything to you about getting married, did he?"

"Getting married! You're crazy."

"Well, your father and my father were working on arrowheads, and I came up to watch. Crashing Thunder said, 'I suppose it won't be long before you boys will be thinking of getting married. It's high time you began to get started in life. You know you can't go on war parties or take part in dances until you get your manitos.'"

"Now what made him joke about getting married, I wonder," Half Sky said.

"I have it." Big Face nodded his head. "Yes, that's it. He must have heard about our giving those little crows to Startled Faun and Little Perch. You know they tamed them and taught them to say, 'Nind ubimin.'"

"You're right. That's what started it. You can't give a girl a pleasant look around this Birch Island but some nosey squaw starts to gossip. That's just like my father to joke about it."

"We might as well get ready for the way everyone will treat us until we go to Dreamer's Rock—just as though we were skunks—or worse." Big Face shook his head.

"They do it to fool the wicked spirits, for if our fathers and mothers act as though we don't amount to much, the wicked spirits will think we aren't worth bothering with."

"Yes, I know," Big Face answered, "but I don't like these days of the fast at all."

They walked toward the village in silence, and it seemed to them that the cooking pots had never given off such delicious smells.

"See you tomorrow," Big Face said as he left Half Sky at the chief's house.

When Half Sky went inside, his mother did not look at him. She scowled when he went near the cooking pot, and he found instead of his soft bearskin bed an old mangy deerhide, stiff and hard. With a sigh he lay down on it and tried to forget food.

In the morning his father called gruffly, "Well, lazy one, aren't you going to get your worthless carcass out of my way?"

Half Sky knew very well that his father and mother loved him and that their harsh words were spoken to fool the good as well as the evil spirits. When a good spirit sees a boy whose parents are cross to him, this kind power takes pity on the child and helps more than usual. Crashing Thunder and Flying Cloud were trying to get all the help they could for their son.

So Half Sky tried not to feel bad when his father called him "worthless" or "flea-bitten"; nor did he think his mother cruel when she gave him only a crust of burned bread. He knew this was all a part of finding his manito, but he did not like it, and he hurried to see how Big Face was feeling.

As he came to Big Face's tepee he saw his friend come running out of the doorway with his mother close behind. She flourished a stick of firewood and cried, "Don't come back today. We don't want you."

The two boys stood staring at each other. "This finding one's manito is getting rough," Big Face said. "She ran me out of my own tepee."

"Just think how sorry the good spirit will feel," Half Sky told him. "Besides, our fasting is just about over."

They sauntered down to the canoe landing where they intended to paddle off somewhere by themselves, but Blackbird saw them and called, "Don't take any canoes. We can't trust such rascals as you with even our oldest ones."

To make matters worse, Startled Faun and Little Perch came along giggling, their noses in the air, and went by without speaking. The two boys sat on the rocks by the water and wished the day would end.

"Do you know when we go to Dreamer's Rock?" Big Face asked finally.

"Tomorrow," Half Sky said.

"Thank the Great Spirit! I can't stand much more of this being snubbed by everyone. Let's go home and sleep as soon as the loon begins his night call."

When Half Sky got home there was a little thin soup in a battered old bowl and some more burned bread. He ate them, and lay down on the stiff old deerskin. At dawn when he got up his father offered him a bowl of water. He drank it and smeared ashes from the cooking fire over himself.

"You know where to go," his father said. "You will find a canoe you and Big Face can use. At Dreamer's Rock, you must separate and not see each other except evenings. You know you must not eat or drink while the sun is in the sky. I will come each day and bring water. Be sure to remember your dreams and tell me when I come. May your manito show himself to you soon."

Without a backward look Half Sky walked to the canoe landing where he saw Big Face also smeared with ashes. They got into the canoe that Blackbird had ready. He shoved them off. Over the blue water they skimmed, and soon the sheer cliff of Dreamer's Rock loomed in front of them. After tying the canoe, they parted. Half Sky took one path; Big Face the other.

CHAPTER 9

Dreamer's Rock

HALF SKY climbed up the steep path until he reached a great flat rock, level and smooth. An overhanging shelf jutted out and made a shelter from sudden rain. After he had cut cedar boughs and made himself a soft bed, he lay down and looked over the bay.

He breathed the spicy fragrance. He thought of how many of his tribe had lain on this white rock and had found their manitos. Hungry and thirsty, he looked down on the sparkling blue water that rolled down the bay and dashed against the rocks of Birch Island. How he wished he had a drink of that clear, cold water.

To forget his hunger and thirst, he began to listen to sounds—the ha-ha, ha-ha of the loons as they tumbled about on the white-crested waves that rolled in from Quartz Rock, the screams of the gulls as they fought over an unlucky little perch, and the rap, rap, tappity, tap of the woodpeckers. Luckily his scrambling over the rocks and his fasting had made him tired. He fell asleep.

When he awoke at evening, Crashing Thunder stood by him with a skin bag of water and a small piece of blueberry bread. Half Sky drank gratefully and ate the bread in two mouthfuls.

"Have you seen anything?" his father asked. "Has no one come to you in a dream?"

"No," Half Sky said sadly.

"Pray to the Good Spirit. Perhaps tomorrow night you will have good news for me." Crashing Thunder walked down the steep path, and soon Half Sky saw his father's canoe darting back to Birch Island. He thought about his father's care for him, about the danger from the Iroquois, about his mother and sister, about Grandfather Footsteps of the Bear. He was ashamed but he always came back to thinking of his mother's wonderful cooking.

He knew his carefree days were over, and he prayed to the Great Spirit to send him a helper, a guardian spirit who would guide him. He slept little that night, for the water kept saying, "Warfare, warfare." The wind blew fitfully. It seemed that he heard people talking. He could almost catch the words, then the wind blew them away. He could hear soft footsteps on the rocks. He was very hungry.

As the grayness of dawn began to come, he thought how sad his father would be that the night had brought no dream. A disgrace to the Ojibways, he was, and he a chief's son! How he wished he could see Big Face. What if no dream ever came? Tears sprang into his eyes, and he turned over on his cedar bed with the hope that changing his position might bring better luck.

As the light became better he saw, growing out of the cracks of the rock, tiny plants bearing little bell-like yellow flowers. Just beyond them tall stalks of great flamelike blossoms bent in the wind. All about these blooms hummingbirds darted. Their wings whirred so swiftly that the birds seemed to be standing still in the air.

He was almost dizzy watching them, and somehow he began to feel encouraged. Then just as suddenly he was discouraged again. Perhaps he was the black sheep of the village. He was almost sure he would never find his manito. He thought he would go home, but then he remembered his father's advice to pray to the Good Spirit. He used the prayer his grandfather had taught him.

> "Great Spirit, Master of our lives,
> Great Spirit, Master of all things—visible and invisible,
> Command the good spirits to help me,
> Keep at a distance all evil ones.
> Help our courage and our strength."

He went to sleep repeating his prayer. He dreamed that he was sitting in a forest of flame-colored trees where hundreds and hundreds of hummingbirds were dancing to the music of acorn drums. He could see the drummers tapping out the tune with their long bills. Tum, tum, tum, tummity, tum. A quick, jolly tune. Over and over they played it until Half Sky knew it by heart.

It was different from any other song he had ever heard. He found himself singing it and tapping out the rhythm with his fingers. No longer was he worried. So glad was he that he began to chant the age-old welcome to the rising sun.

"Take heart, Ojibways,
The Great Spirit has sent the glorious Sun;
Be of good cheer, my brothers,

The Great Spirit sends another day.
How great are the works of the Spirit of Goodness.
He sets the water in motion,
He makes the corn grow, the children and old ones to rejoice.
Take heart, the Sun brings another day."

As Half Sky finished his prayer, he had an odd feeling that he was falling down and down. When he came to rest on soft moss, he found he was no bigger than a hummingbird. The drummers swung into a livelier tune, and as they beat faster and faster, the birds stopped dancing. They milled about Half Sky, and he found himself in the middle of a round-domed chief's house like his father's. It was made of hummingbirds packed together, wing overlapping wing like a thatched roof. Even the curtain at the doorway was of hummingbirds.

As he watched, someone outside lifted the feathered curtain. Half Sky stared. "Nind ubimin. Nind ubimin," he said faintly. How lucky for him that he had remembered his manners.

In walked a gorgeous creature with a feathered headdress of rainbow colors. Under one wing he carried a war club. Why, he's a hummingbird, Half Sky thought, as the shining one skimmed up to the boy.

"Here it is," said the hummingbird. He gave Half Sky a tiny acorn drum, a packet of sweet-smelling herbs wrapped in deerskin, and the war club.

"I will be your protector," he told Half Sky. "Whenever you are in trouble, beat the acorn drum."

Half Sky awoke, looked about him, and went to sleep again.

He dreamed the same dream once more. Now the talking water and the wind rushing through the pines blended with the tune played by the hummingbird drummers. Something touched him.

He awoke to find his father standing at his side. Crashing Thunder gave him broiled venison and water. Even though he was hungry, Half Sky wanted to tell his father about his dream right away.

"No," his father said, "eat. And don't tell me all about the dream. It is enough to know you have found your manito. You must tell no one but Herb Gatherer what happened to you. The Great Spirit be praised."

After Half Sky had drunk the water and eaten the venison, he said, "My manito is a hummingbird."

"Good." Crashing Thunder smiled. "But what is that you have in your hand?"

"In my hand?" Half Sky held out his palm and stared at the acorn. "Why—why . . ."

Just then from above them floated down a single feather of the golden eagle. It came to rest on Half Sky's head. For some reason he was frightened.

"Don't be scared," Crashing Thunder said. "You are lucky. The hummingbirds—not one but many—and the feather. Now we will go back to the Island where we will ask the Herb Gatherer to tell what your dream means."

Half Sky was so faint that he slipped and slid down the rocky path, but finally he reached the water. He washed off the ashes from his face and stepped into the canoe. "Found your manito. Found your manito. Found your manito," the water sang as Crashing Thunder paddled the canoe toward Birch Island.

Just behind were Big Face and his father. Big Face, too, thought Half Sky, must have found his manito, for he looked happy. The boys nodded but were too awed to speak.

Half Sky watched the blue water as it swirled about Dreamer's Rock and later foamed against the rocky headland of Birch Island. With the dream very real, he scarcely heard the pebbles grate underneath as his father landed. Almost immediately the air was full of the delicious smell of broiling venison and corn soup.

As he neared home, he saw blueberry bread beside the cooking fire. With delight Flying Cloud filled and refilled his bowl, a beautiful new one made of curly grained wood. She broke off enormous hunks of hot bread and gave him sweet bear oil to eat with it. He drank a whole bowlful of soup at once. He stopped eating only long enough to say, "Oongh ondjita. Mother, you are a wonderful cook."

"Keep your eyes open for a girl who can cook like your mother," Crashing Thunder advised.

There it was again—talking about girls. He'd settle this once and for all. "I don't want any girl's cooking. I don't want ever to get married. I want to stay here always," Half Sky told them. "Unless you want to get rid of me."

Crashing Thunder and Flying Cloud looked at each other and smiled. "Of course, of course," his father said, "we'll be glad to have you here. We're proud of you, but when you dress up in your new clothes—well, you'll have to take care of yourself, that's all. Well, Half Sky, what do you say we go to

Herb Gatherer's right now? Do you have your acorn and feather?"

As they walked together, Half Sky realized that as soon as a young man found his manito, it was polite to joke him about getting married. His mother and father were letting him know that when a boy finds his manito, he is no longer a child.

When they reached Herb Gatherer's, Crashing Thunder lifted the doorway curtain.

"Nind ubimin. Nind ubimin. Come in, Crashing Thunder and Half Sky."

"How did you know who it was?" Half Sky asked.

"I dreamed about you," Herb Gatherer said. "I expected you. Now sit on this cedar mat, make yourself comfortable, and tell everything that happened."

Crashing Thunder went outside, for it was not right that anyone except a medicine man should hear all that had happened. When Half Sky told of the dome-shaped hut made of hummingbirds, Herb Gatherer nodded. When Half Sky explained how the gaily dressed bird creature had said, "Here it is," and held out the war club, the sweet herbs and the acorn drum, Herb Gatherer's eyes sparkled.

The story of how the single eagle feather had alighted on Half Sky's head brought "Hah, good," from the medicine man. Herb Gatherer sat watching the boy with eyes that glowed.

"Here is the acorn I found in my hand when I woke up. I don't know how I got it."

"Why, it's been hollowed out and there is a sort of covering over the end of it," the medicine man said. He looked

first at the acorn and then at Half Sky. "I must think a bit,"
he mumbled. "I must consult my manito. Very odd. Very
odd."

He dropped twelve pinches of tobacco on his cooking fire.
Half Sky watched the white smoke as it swirled about the
tepee and finally drifted out through the hole in the roof.

"The hummingbird dream is good," Herb Gatherer said.
"You will never be killed by arrows. You will always come
back safe from the wars. You should take the hummingbird
as your manito and wear one in your crest when you go into
battle. You must offer tobacco to your manito when you are
in trouble. You should have the hummingbird tattooed on
your chest.

"The dome-shaped house of hummingbirds means you will
be a great chief and a fortunate one. The tune you heard on
the acorn drum is your special song. You must practice it
often. You must listen for your manito to give you the words,
for you will have to sing them at the next great feast."

"What does the eagle feather mean?"

"You will be called on to lead another tribe besides your
own, and you must begin to study other tongues. No longer
can you be a boy. This eagle feather is a sign of destiny."

"What shall I do with this acorn?"

"If you will let me take it and the eagle feather, I will make
a little medicine bundle for you to carry about with you always. Raise the doorway curtain. I have done."

Crashing Thunder came in and set down before Herb Gatherer a bearskin robe, a green necklace, and two white deerskin
summer robes. He handed Half Sky an otter-skin pouch of

The white smoke swirled about the tepee

tobacco to give to the medicine man. Herb Gatherer sat with closed eyes, swaying gently. Father and son stepped out quietly.

"Put the stick against the door, will you?" asked Herb Gatherer. "I must think, and I don't want to be disturbed."

As they walked homeward, Crashing Thunder said, "Perhaps you'd like to be alone so you can find the words for your tune."

Half Sky left his father and sat on the rocky ledge. Here many times he had watched through the clear water the big bass lying among the rocks. Here he had decided such silly things as whether to go fishing or swimming.

For a long time he listened to the tune that the humming-bird drummer had taught him. It beat in his ears. Tum, tum, tummity, tum. An odd tune but a steady one. Words, however, would not come. He sat and thought and thought. Not one word came. He had decided he might as well go home when Big Face came walking along the rocks and sat down beside him.

"Did you find your manito, Half Sky?"

"Yes. A hummingbird. What's yours?"

"A loon. At first I was scared. I was afraid a loon might be bad luck, but Herb Gatherer says it's all right. We are not supposed to tell everything that happened, are we?"

"No," said Half Sky. He was glad he did not have to, because he did not want Big Face to think he was talking big.

"Now, we should go to Footsteps of the Bear and to other older men and ask for lessons. Herb Gatherer said we have much to learn and not too much time to do it," Big Face said.

"Did he tell you that, too?" Half Sky wondered what Herb Gatherer meant.

"Do you know I am to be the fish caller?" Big Face asked. "I have to practice every day. I must say before I go fishing, 'Oh, my brothers, you fish who swim around Birch Island, allow yourselves to be caught by us Ojibways. We will give your bones honorable burial. We will promise never to burn them. Come and be caught by your friends.' "

When the two boys came to Grandfather Footsteps of the Bear's tepee, they found him outside making a snare for a bear. He listened eagerly to Half Sky's news that he and Big Face had found their manitos.

"And," Half Sky added, "Herb Gatherer says we should study under you."

"Let's begin now," Grandfather said. "I think you know such simple things as getting through woods and dry leaves without noise. You know how the wind betrays the hunter, too. I have taught you to make snares like this." He held up the bear snare.

"But now you must learn about deer tracks and how to tell whether the deer is young or old, buck or doe. You must know the time of year when deer may be hunted, and the time of day when deer are most likely to rest or be on the feeding grounds."

"Big Face is to be a fish caller," Half Sky told Grandfather.

"Well, then Big Face must learn about fish—when the bass spawn, when the sturgeon, when the pike, and where.

"While you are here, you might look at this bear snare. I don't like to hunt bear now because I can't climb a tree as fast as I used to."

Both boys looked at the snare and each made one. It was growing late, and cooking smells all over the village evidenced it was time to eat. Each boy hurried to the forest to set his bear snare. Twilight was coming on when they returned, and Half Sky and Big Face ran home for a hot supper.

CHAPTER 10

A Song at Last

HALF SKY woke up with the tum-tummity-tum tune to which the hummingbirds had danced sounding in his ears. Tum, tum tummity-tum, the beats of the acorn drum thrummed and thrummed; he could not get rid of it. All night its haunting rhythm had not left him.

He looked about for his mother, then he remembered that she and White Goose had gone to gather the green-and-white striped squashes. He got up from his bearskin bed and sniffed. What has Mother left in the cooking pot for my breakfast? A stew, that's what. Red beans, little cubes of squash, and dried fish! "Good!" he said as he dished out a bowlful and sat down on the floor to eat it.

What a wonderful planner his mother was. Just like a squirrel hoarding for winter. Overhead from the poles hung bags of dried blueberries, raspberries, and tangy wild plums. Ears of rainbow-colored hard corn, braided together, were tied all about. Strings of wild potatoes that had been boiled, then dried in the sun, festooned the side poles. The grease bags were full.

Directly overhead he saw the bag he especially liked. It held the marrow that his mother had scooped out of the bones of bear and moose. How often had he watched her crack the bones and throw the marrow into the cooking pot. When all was melted she poured it into the skin bag for winter. How good it would taste on blueberry bread when the snow drifted about his home and the waters about Birch Island were so solid that he and Big Face could play hockey in the winter sunshine away out in the bay. Certainly, Flying Cloud was getting ready for winter. Something very comforting, Half Sky thought, to sit with a full stomach and gloat on food to eat when the north wind puffed and blew the smoke back through the smoke hole.

Peeking outside, he could see his father sharpening arrowheads. Crashing Thunder hummed an endless tune as his fingers went back and forth over the sharp flint. Last night there had been talk of a wild-duck hunt. It did not seem possible that the redheaded ducklings that had skittered over the summer water had grown big enough to hunt.

Half Sky was not especially interested in hunting. The Great Feast filled his mind. Everyone expected him to get up and sing his song at that time. Not one word of song had come to him. What if he, the chief's son, stood as silly as a crane on the day of the big feast with no song? He shook his head and walked outside.

"Hey," his father called, without looking up, "what do you think you are going to do today, Chief Half Sky?"

"I don't know. Somehow I . . ."

Crashing Thunder looked up. "What ails you?"

"Well, I just can't get a song to go with the tune I dreamed. Here the Great Feast is near, my new clothes ready, and I with no song. What shall I do?"

"Hah, hah," said Crashing Thunder as he dropped his arrowhead and looked over the blue water. "Now, let's see. If I were you, I'd go to one of those lonesome islands out in the bay there. I'd make a little fire and I'd burn tobacco to my manito. Then I'd pray. Then you can get yourself a song. I think perhaps you had better see Herb Gatherer."

Half Sky nodded and walked toward Herb Gatherer's tepee. The medicine man was sitting outside making hunting charms.

"I am glad to see the Great Spirit has given you another day," Half Sky said politely.

"And I pray Him to grant you long life and, above all, happiness," Herb Gatherer answered. After a pause he said, "Still worrying about that song? Sometimes they come hard. What does Crashing Thunder advise?"

"To go to one of those islands out there, make a fire, burn tobacco to the manito, and wait. He said to ask you."

"Yes, yes, go to an island and pray, but take this."

He handed Half Sky a small deerskin package, so small it could be carried in the shoulder pouch. When he opened it, Half Sky saw a little acorn drum, but instead of a drumhead made of spider web, it had over the end a thin one of skin, a tiny drum beater, a little envelope of sweet herbs, and the golden eagle feather fastened to the deerskin case by porcupine quills. Alongside lay a miniature tobacco pouch.

Half Sky's eyes brightened. "My medicine bundle?"

Herb Gatherer nodded.

"I feel better already, Herb Gatherer. I thank you."

"Go find your song," the medicine man advised as he began again to work on his hunting charms.

Half Sky ran to the landing place, took a canoe and, after pushing it off the gravelly slope, jumped in and knelt, paddle in his hand. A few strokes took him away from Birch Island. He stopped for a few minutes to make up his mind which rocky island to go to. Then he noticed the wind was taking him straight toward Dreamer's Rock.

"Of course," he said, "that's where my manito wants me to go. I'll find the fireweed, and perhaps my guardian spirit, the hummingbird, the whirring one, will be there."

He did not have to paddle at all, for the wind pushed the light canoe quickly down the bay. He reached the great cliff of Dreamer's Rock and guided his craft into the little harbor, jumped out onto a white rock, and drew his canoe up out of the water.

Scrambling up the rocky path to the big flat top of the rocky island, he saw the cedar boughs under the shelving rock just as he had left them. Around the flame-colored fireweeds hummingbirds flew about. As he stood there watching them, he opened his medicine bundle and looked at the little acorn drum.

"You will never get your song here," a squeaky little voice said. "You must listen to the water. Go down and sit by the shore."

Down he climbed. From his shoulder pouch he took his fire sticks, gathered a little dry wood, and some flimsy white birch bark. Soon he had a little fire. Pinch by pinch he dropped the tobacco on the blaze.

"I am calling on you, my manito. I need help. I have the tune, a good and lively tune. Listen. Tum, tum, tummity-tum. I need words to make a song to celebrate you, my guardian, at the Great Feast. It is almost here, but I have no song. I offer you tobacco. Give me a song, and I will sing of you to all the tribe at the Great Feast."

Hither and thither flashed the hummingbirds; the blue water began to talk, softly at first, then louder and louder. His worries left Half Sky. He had not felt so comfortable in a long time. He stretched out in the warm sunshine. Now and then he thought he could pick out a word or two the water spoke. Then again it sounded as though many people were jabbering a long way off.

Suddenly he sat up. "Small but mighty." Yes, he heard those words. "Small but mighty," he repeated. Then he heard, "Helpers—hard to see us."

He listened carefully, scarcely breathing; the disjointed words made themselves into a song that fitted the tune:

> "We, your helpers, small but mighty,
> Whirring round we all things see,
> Always near you when you need us,
> When you call, we bring blessings."

"That's it. That's it!" Half Sky cried. "I have my song. It doesn't seem possible." He sang it loudly.

"O my guardian spirit," he said when he had finished, "it was as you told me. I learned it from the water."

He could hardly wait to get into the canoe and paddle back against the wind to Birch Island. As soon as he pulled the canoe up on shore he hurried to Herb Gatherer's tepee. He raised the skin flap at the doorway.

"Nind ubimin, Nind ubimin. Come in. I am at home," he heard.

Stepping inside, Half Sky blurted out, "I've found my song. I've found my song. The water taught it to me. Listen:

> *"We, your helpers, small but mighty,*
> *Whirring round we all things see.*
> *Always near you when you need us,*
> *When you call, we bring blessings."*

"A good song," Herb Gatherer said. "You must practice singing it as you dance. You must shake the rattle and keep time to the beat of the drum."

Suddenly the medicine man jumped to his feet. He seemed to be listening to something. "Come, Half Sky. Come. Grandfather Footsteps of the Bear is on his way to the Land of Souls."

Herb Gatherer ran out of the tepee, and Half Sky stumbled after him.

"How do you know? How do you know?" Half Sky kept asking. Herb Gatherer did not answer. He was running toward Grandfather Footsteps of the Bear's tepee.

CHAPTER 11

Sadness

WHEN THEY reached Grandfather's tepee, Herb Gatherer rushed in without waiting for the welcoming words. Grandfather lay on his bearskin mat.

"Why, he's all right, Herb Gatherer, he's smiling at me," Half Sky said.

Herb Gatherer dropped to his knees and bent over Grandfather Footsteps of the Bear. The medicine man lifted Grandfather's wrist. "I'm afraid he's gone. The old chief will never sound the alarm again on the Bell Rocks. He is on his way to the Land of Souls. Half Sky, go tell your father."

The boy tried to say something but his lips were stiff. "Oh, Grandfather," he whispered.

"Go get your father," Herb Gatherer reminded him. Half Sky stumbled out of the tepee. He couldn't believe his grandfather was dead. Why, only last night Grandfather had said, "Tomorrow, Half Sky, you and Big Face must start your deer-tracking lesson."

Half Sky stumbled on, his tears blurring the path. He almost ran into his father. "Come," he said. "Grandfather . . ." He could say no more but followed Crashing Thunder.

As he followed his father through the open doorway into the old chief's tepee, he saw that Herb Gatherer had already found the best robe and was wrapping Footsteps of the Bear in it. Now Crashing Thunder and the medicine man laid the old chief on his side with his knees drawn up to his breast. Herb Gatherer opened his medicine pouch and took out a little packet of red ointment. After he had rubbed the soles of Grandfather's feet with the red oil, he put the new moccasins on him.

"Take courage, O Footsteps of the Bear," Herb Gatherer said in a low voice as though Grandfather could hear. "Without fear as always, make your way through the Great Meadow. Your father, mother, son, and warrior friends are waiting for you. They are anxious to see you. Soon all of us will follow you. Give your blessing to Half Sky, for he loved you."

Crashing Thunder sent the crier out to tell all the Birch Islanders that the old chief had started on his long journey to the Spirit Land. Half Sky crouched in a corner of his grandfather's tepee and thought of the arrows and drums he had watched Foosteps of the Bear make, of the jokes, the war stories, and the prayers he had learned in this tepee.

Blackbird came and told of the old chief's wisdom and bravery in battle. "Come, Half Sky," he said, "you should be proud of your grandfather. He was a great Ojibway."

Half Sky nodded. Nothing mattered now. All he could think of was that he had lost his good friend.

Everything that Footsteps of the Bear owned, his bowl and spoon, his feathered headdress, his fire sticks, his bows and arrows, his medicine bundle, his tomahawk, Crashing Thunder laid at Grandfather's feet. His war club, however, that had passed from chief to chief, the magic club used to sound the Ojibway alarm on the Bell Rocks, Crashing Thunder kept.

Crow Tongue began a sorrowful song

"As I take this war club today, so, Half Sky, you must take it when I leave for the Land of Souls. I pray I may make as good use of it as did Footsteps of the Bear. And so, Half Sky, you must pray, too." He touched his son lightly with the war club. Suddenly the hopeless feeling passed, and Half Sky's eyes lighted. He felt closer to his father than he ever had before.

Flying Cloud came in with Crow Tongue and took her place near the old chief. Crow Tongue began a sorrowful song. Other women crowded in, and when Crow Tongue wept, all the other women wailed. When she sang, they sang. All night they mourned. Warriors passed in and out of the tepee. Outside, friends played sticks and spoke of the great wisdom of Footsteps of the Bear. Above all, the old men told of Footsteps of the Bear's kindness in giving of his food when game was scarce. No warrior shed a tear; they left the weeping for the women.

Soon the presents began to come—a new cedar mat and a piece of birch bark to shelter the body of Footsteps of the Bear from the weather, an elkskin robe embroidered with porcupine quills, a fat grease bag to help in the funeral feast.

Half Sky tried to be brave, and when Big Face came, the two boys tried to think of something to help Grandfather in his long journey to the Great Meadow. They decided to make a bear trap, the finest one ever made. For Grandfather had taught them and what could be better than to make him one to take on his lonesome way? Together they worked all night and day, and at last, when they brought in the trap, Crashing Thunder and Herb Gatherer said, "Good. Nothing will Footsteps of the Bear treasure more." The boys felt proud and somehow they felt older.

At last came the day of the funeral, and Grandfather's old friends carried the body out through a window. Half Sky knew that if they took Grandfather through the doorway, it would be inviting others to go to the Spirit Land. Half Sky thought he could not bear it when the warriors laid Grandfather in the grave along with all his possessions.

In each cooking pot they made a small hole so the spirit of the cooking pot could go to the Land of Souls with Grandfather. Each ax was broken, each arrow chipped, everything was "killed" so the spirits of the ax, the arrow, the traps could go along with Grandfather's spirit as he made his way to the Great Meadow, the Happy Hunting Ground.

While the cooking pots, arrows, axes and traps were being arranged, Crashing Thunder, Half Sky, Flying Cloud, and White Goose chanted the old chief's deeds. All the time they sang, they swung slender rods to which they had tied little bells. These jingled mournfully. Now and then they touched the bear totem, head downward at the head of the grave.

All the Birch Islanders followed the old chief to his grave, and the head of each family threw a handful of dust into it. When the cedar mats and birch-bark strips were laid on top, everyone turned toward home.

Just as the funeral party started to go back to the village, Crow Tongue's Iroquois slave and many women came with broiled venison, roasted breastbone of bear, cooking pots full of fish and parched corn. Everyone took a small bit of meat and dropped it into the hole left at the head of the grave.

Half Sky stepped into a dark cedar thicket until the villagers had left. He sat down on a log. His eyes filled with tears. He knew he wasn't acting like a warrior, but he had loved his grandfather and missed him. It was going to be hard not to see him. Besides he was alone and didn't need to pretend to be brave any longer.

Someone touched his arm. He jumped. Turning he saw Big Face.

"Half Sky," his friend began, then his voice broke. "Half Sky," he tried again. "If we turn out to be only a quarter as good as your grandfather, we'll . . ."

He swallowed hard. The two boys looked at each other and nodded. Darkness came but they still sat there. Afar off they heard twigs snap.

"Half Sky! Half Sky!" someone called. The voice was low and muted. Not like anything they had ever heard unless— unless it was Grandfather.

Come to think of it, they had heard him call just this way. Big Face grasped Half Sky's hand. "Are you scared?" he whispered.

Before Half Sky could answer, Crashing Thunder loomed in front of them. "Come home, Half Sky. I wondered why you hadn't come. Oh, are you here, Big Face? Better come back with us." As the three walked slowly back to the village, Crashing Thunder pretended he did not know of their tears. As they reached the village, he said, "I know how you feel, but you must take your places at the funeral feast."

"I can't eat," Half Sky said. "I don't want to feast."

"Nor I," Big Face added.

"As I said," Crashing Thunder continued patiently, "you

must both come to the feast. It is in honor of Grandfather Footsteps of the Bear, and some of the food is to help him on his journey. If you do not eat, he cannot. You wouldn't ask him to walk a long way without food, would you?"

As they drew near Crashing Thunder's house, he said, "Why don't you boys rub charcoal over your faces?" He pointed to some charcoal; they knew what he meant. With their faces smeared with black, no one could see they had been crying. Gratefully they blackened themselves and went inside.

The visitors from other villages stayed several days, and Flying Cloud's food was being eaten fast. Besides, Crashing Thunder had to find presents for everyone who brought a gift for Footsteps of the Bear. Finally, when the last visitor had gone, Flying Cloud said anxiously, "My husband, my grease bag is empty; my meat shelf bare; my dried fish almost gone."

Crashing Thunder said, "It is true that the chief is the poorest man in the village because he has to feed and give presents to everyone. I have nothing left. Even my beads are gone. And here is Half Sky ready for his first Great Feast as a young warrior, and we have no clothes for him. We had to give the deerskin robes, the leggings, the . . ."

"I hope you won't scold, Crashing Thunder, but I have all of Half Sky's new clothes ready. I—I hid them. But I don't think I did wrong, because they wouldn't fit anyone else."

Crashing Thunder said nothing, and Flying Cloud was relieved.

Life settled down again in Birch Island, and the women gathered nuts, hunted for wild potatoes to dry, and urged the men to go fishing. The supply of dried whitefish was about gone. Men and boys went out every day, and each night the birchwood smoke curled up from fish-smoking fires. Venison was cut in narrow strips and smoked; the fat from moose and bear was tried out and poured into grease bags.

The nights were cold now, and the wind howled around the tepees. Flying Cloud rummaged through her baskets to find Crashing Thunder's leggings and robe. One night after supper she brought out the new clothes Half Sky would wear to the Great Feast where he must sing his song. There was a new breechcloth with red and yellow quills on the flaps that hung down in front and back. The leggings had deep red borders and long fringe at the sides. The moccasins were decorated with red-deer hair. A robe made of buckskin had a bear fashioned of porcupine quills on the back. The shoulder pocket of dyed deerskin especially pleased Half Sky.

"Oh, Mother," he said, "I thought you had given away my new clothes. Now I can sing of my hummingbird helper and look as grand as he did."

"Tomorrow," said Crashing Thunder, "we men must put up the Big House for the Great Feast."

"And we women will clean it. I wonder where we can get good dry grass to sit on. Have you seen any, my husband?"

"Yes, Half Sky can take you there tomorrow and you can take Crow Tongue's Iroquois along to help. Then we will have to make the sweat tent, Half Sky, so we will all be clean for the Great Feast."

Half Sky drifted off to sleep thinking of a hummingbird dressed in a ceremonial robe, of singing the song before all the people, of new clothes, and of all things, Crow Tongue's Iroquois. He looked up at his medicine bundle that he had hung on a tent pole so it would not touch the ground. For some reason he felt uneasy.

But tonight there was a difference. He had seen a great change come into his life, and he knew that other changes would come. Somehow he was not afraid, for the same power that had guided Grandfather would guide him. He slept.

CHAPTER 12

One-Who-Guards-and-Warns-of-Danger

"WHIP POOR will! Whip poor will! Whip poor will!" The sound was almost next to Half Sky's ear. The grayness of dawn made it hard to see clearly. "Whip poor will, whip poor will," came from above. Why, that bird must be on top of the cabin! He'd chase him away.

As Half Sky got up from his bearskin bed, he saw that his father's sleeping mat was empty. He wanted to talk to his father. That whippoorwill was unlucky.

Outside, Half Sky stood still and peered into the foggy gray. Where was his father? Hunched over the rocky ledge, a dark shape that must be Crashing Thunder sat as still as the rocks. Half Sky wanted to see whether he was praying and burning tobacco to his manito. It would be impolite to break in on anyone praying. The shape did not move, and as Half Sky came nearer, he saw that Crashing Thunder was staring out over the water.

"Father," Half Sky said, "I want to talk to you."

Crashing Thunder turned. "Come." He pointed to a flat rock.

"That whippoorwill sounded so loud in my ears. I never heard one so shrill."

"A whippoorwill? Where? I didn't hear one. You must have dreamed it. Hah! Whippoorwill! Hah!"

"It's unlucky, Grandfather said," Half Sky whispered.

"Hah. A whippoorwill," muttered Crashing Thunder, looking about.

"I just couldn't sleep. I kept thinking of Grandfather and about the stories of his war club, One-who-guards-and-warns-of-danger. He used to tell me about how first his grandfather owned it, and then his father, and he said when he was gone you would have it, and then I. And then the whippoorwill screeched—but not like a whippoorwill. Couldn't you sleep either, Father?"

"Half Sky, some day if the Good Manito wills, you will be chief. You will have the whole village to worry about. As soon as the Great Feast is over, we must move to Manitoulin. I am afraid we should have gone earlier. There on Manitoulin, we can join with other villages and be stronger to fight off any Iroquois war parties. I hear the Sioux are raiding, too."

"Where have you put the One-who-guards-and-warns-of-danger? It's a magic war club, isn't it, Father?"

"It's right over my sleeping place. I will watch it."

"Whip poor will, whip poor will," sounded first from the forest, then from the chief's cabin.

A shrill scream sent Crashing Thunder and Half Sky running toward home. They heard Flying Cloud call and White Goose crying. Smoke poured out of the cabin, and through it Half Sky made out two or three skulking figures.

An Iroquois was dragging Flying Cloud away. Crashing Thunder rushed up and raised his tomahawk. At that moment a shape jumped out of the smoke and struck the chief. Both men fell together. Half Sky picked up a big rock and brought it down on the one who had hit his father.

"The war club! One-who-guards-and-warns-of-danger," Crashing Thunder whispered.

Half Sky rushed into the cabin. The magic club was gone. He heard his mother scream again and he turned to see someone pulling her toward a canoe at the landing place. As he ran toward the beach, someone hit him a glancing blow with a war club. When his head cleared, he saw the canoe was already far from the island. Over the water came the mocking call, "Whip poor will. Whip poor will."

"Mother, Mother!" Half Sky screamed.

"Whip poor will. Whip poor will," was his answer.

With a throbbing head he hurried toward the burning cabin where the islanders were running about in all directions. He saw his father stretched out on a flat rock and Herb Gatherer bending over him.

Blackbird, Big Face, and others were trying to find Flying Cloud and White Goose in the smoke-filled cabin.

"They're gone!" Half Sky shouted. "I saw warriors take them in a canoe. They have taken Grandfather's club, too."

"Flying Cloud? White Goose?" Crashing Thunder struggled to get up. "Whippoorwill. Flying Cloud, White Goose," he kept saying. "Got to find . . ."

"You stay right here," Herb Gatherer said. "Lie still. Blackbird is getting warriors to go after Flying Cloud and White Goose."

"Water, water, water to put out the fire," someone shouted. The women and children were filling bark pails with water.

Men grabbed cooking pots and ran to the shore to fill them and throw the water on the fire. At last they had the blaze under control.

Besides watching Crashing Thunder, Herb Gatherer had been busy spreading salve on those who had been burned.

Suddenly the chief opened his eyes and started to fling his arms about. "I must find Flying Cloud and White Goose. I must bring back One-who-guards-and-warns-of-danger," he said over and over.

"Just lie still," Herb Gatherer told him. "Blackbird is rounding up warriors to bring back Flying Cloud."

West Wind came up. "It looks as if what the Iroquois wanted this time was the chief's war club. Crow Tongue's slave and the other Iroquois are gone. Hah! They didn't stay to fight it out. Steal and run. Just like Iroquois dogs."

Half Sky found his head had stopped aching, and he hurried to the poles the men had put up for the Great Feast. Drums boomed. The Ojibway war chant sounded, low and menacing. Equipped with bows, arrows, and war clubs, the villagers began to dance about the pole, slowly at first, then faster and faster.

Some were already painted with red and yellow stripes between broad bands of black. Others were decorating themselves. Big Face had the most wonderful paint job of any warrior in the village. When he saw Half Sky without any paint, he yelled, "Where's your paint? You look like a ghost."

He began to smear Half Sky with brilliant red and yellow.

Crashing Thunder called his son to him. "Don't rest," he said, "until you find Flying Cloud, White Goose, and the

One-who-guards. Bring them back. Remember you can honor Footsteps of the Bear the way he would wish. Be sure to call on your manito."

"We have thirty warriors," Blackbird was saying. "We must all eat quickly. It's easier to carry food in the stomach than in the shoulder pocket. Fill your bags with parched corn. We have no time to waste. I think the raiders are the same ones we put to rout by the drums. This time we cannot use tricks. We must fight. Hah! Now we eat."

As soon as the cooking pots were empty, Blackbird stood up. "Great Spirit," he said, "we thank you that you told us to put rocks in the canoes and sink them in a hidden place last night."

Everyone helped raise the hidden canoes and empty out the stones. Blackbird used Crashing Thunder's canoe with the red-and-yellow thunderbird painted on it. He was just about to give the signal to dip paddles when West Wind called, "Where are we going?"

"To Burnt Island," Blackbird answered. "They carried one dead warrior away, for I saw him. They will bury him on Burnt Island. That's where they always put their dead."

"Wait a minute, Blackbird, I don't believe they will go as far as that," said West Wind. "They are hoping we will think they are going there. According to what my manito tells me, they will paddle across to the mainland and bury the man there. They'll go by land almost to Iroquois Island. Why not send our best tracker across to the mainland to see whether he can pick up their trail?" West Wind urged.

"Blackbird, send Blackbird," someone called. "He's the best tracker in the tribe."

Blackbird nodded and called Red Hawk. Together they skimmed over the water to the mainland. Everyone watched and waited.

"Here they come back," Half Sky said.

Without getting out of the canoe, Blackbird called, "You don't need to go to Burnt Island. The Iroquois are traveling by land. I know because Flying Cloud was smart enough to drop this bead."

He held up a carnelian bead. "The warriors must be the same ones that got scared by Half Sky's drum. Older men would never have let Flying Cloud mark the trail that way."

"Very likely they are in disgrace, and they're trying to win back their tribe's approval. You don't know what they may take it in their heads to do. Everybody ready?"

Blackbird gave the order and they paddled swiftly to the mainland. Once there, they filled their canoes with rocks and sank them under a low shrubby bank. Blackbird went ahead to search for marks of the trail. Since the forest was dense, he stopped every few steps and examined the shrubs, the trees, the thick layer of pine needles. He shook his head.

As night came on, Blackbird did an almost unheard of thing—he posted a guard. Everyone else curled up under his light robe and slept. For supper, they tightened their belts. "No fires," Blackbird ordered.

Half Sky and Big Face lay down side by side, but neither could sleep. "Why don't you try to hear something?" Big Face whispered. "Half Sky, ask your manito for extra keen ears."

"It's no use." Half Sky sighed. As he lifted his ear from the ground, he said, "I hear nothing. Not even the water talks tonight. I am afraid bad luck will follow me because I did not watch One-who-guards-and-warns-of-danger."

Finally the boys slept. Half Sky dreamed of a hummingbird that whirred around and around his head. It finally lighted on his nose. "Can't you smell anything, my son? Don't rely on your ears alone. Go on until you smell Flying Cloud's corn soup with the secret seasoning. Those young Iroquois whipper-snappers are not wise like Blackbird, who makes you fast to-night so no cooking smells will betray you. Follow your nose! Do you hear, follow your nose." The hummingbird tapped Half Sky's nose so sharply he woke up.

"Follow your nose." Half Sky sniffed. Yes, he thought he could smell meat cooking.

When he told Blackbird of his dream and asked to go alone to see whether the smell grew stronger, the old tracker surprised him by saying, "Your helper has spoken."

"Don't you smell a faint soup smell?" Half Sky asked.

"Well, now you speak of it, I do seem to get a faint supper smell. I wonder. Flying Cloud is smart. Do you think she could have offered to get supper—and then dropped in her secret seasoning that travels far and makes your mouth water? I wonder . . . Your manito doesn't lie."

Half Sky nodded and made sure his shoulder bag was in place.

Blackbird whistled softly and told the guard to let Half Sky go on. "But," he cautioned, "if you do find out any-thing, don't try to be the big hero and do everything alone. Come back and get help."

Everywhere the forest was damp and mossy. Half Sky thought he was walking in a swamp, so squashy were the pine needles. He stepped lightly so he would leave no marks. On and on he crept. Now and then he stopped to listen. The wind, now high in the treetops, swooped down and blew his hair. The faint smell of food made him so hungry he thought he could not go on. No, now the food smell was gone. He was imagining things. Suddenly the delicious fragrance came again. This time he had to reach into his shoulder pouch and take a small pinch of parched corn and tree sugar. Soon afterward he saw the tiny glimmer of a cooking fire.

He dropped to his knees and inched along. He almost put his hands on a sleeping Iroquois. He drew back and sat on the wet pine needles for a long time looking at a little clearing. Near the tiny fire he made out Flying Cloud and White Goose. He was wondering how he was going to wake his mother when she put up her hand and beckoned.

He crept up to her. She was tied to a tree, but Half Sky's flint knife soon cut through the thongs. His mother picked up White Goose and followed Half Sky into the shadows.

Not a word did they say until they reached their own guards. Then Half Sky called softly.

Blackbird appeared from out of the darkness. He greeted Flying Cloud and White Goose. Then to Half Sky, he said, "Did you get the magic club? One-who-guards-and-warns-of-danger?"

The boy felt his face flush. He had been so delighted to find his mother unharmed that he hadn't looked for the war club.

"No," he said slowly. "I didn't look for it. I'm no good as a warrior. What would Grandfather say!"

"Don't take it too hard, Half Sky," Blackbird said. "After

all, you did find your mother and sister. And you didn't wake the sleeping Iroquois."

Flying Cloud laughed. She pointed to a little pouch she carried on a thong around her neck. "Good medicine." She laughed again as she tapped the little bag. "A few pinches of this powder that Herb Gatherer gave me to make sleep was good medicine for Iroquois. Very good."

Blackbird laughed. Half Sky suddenly realized it was not his skill but his mother's shrewdness that had saved her.

"Mother, the reason I didn't wake up the camp was . . ."

"Let well enough alone, my son," she advised. "Thank the Good Manito that everything has turned out well."

"Half Sky," Blackbird said, "take your mother and go down by the canoes and wait for us. With those silly Iroquois as sleepy as they are, we will make sure they don't come chirping around like whippoorwills again."

"You aren't sending me away because I didn't get One-who-guards, are you?"

"No," Blackbird answered shortly. "You did your work. The Great Spirit didn't make us perfect. Take your mother and sister down to the shore."

When Flying Cloud, White Goose, and Half Sky reached the place where the canoes were hidden, they sank down on a birch log and rested. At dawn Blackbird and his warriors appeared and soon had the canoes emptied and ready to start the journey home.

As they came within hailing distance of Birch Island, Blackbird let out the hailing cry and followed it by the death yell seven times repeated. He gave the Ojibway rescue cry twice.

They came within hailing distance of Birch Island

As the halloos echoed and re-echoed over the water, all Birch Island Village streamed to the landing place. They grabbed Flying Cloud, White Goose, and Half Sky and carried them to the new round-domed house they had built for their chief. To Flying Cloud's delight, her cooking pots had not been broken, and many women brought dried fish, bags of marrow, corn meal, and dried squash.

Blackbird came up from the beach. "Come, Half Sky," he said, "let the women admire the new house. We must take One-who-guards-and-warns-of-danger to Crashing Thunder."

"You got it!" Half Sky grinned. "And the Iroquois?" he asked.

"I'm afraid Crow Tongue will have to get along without her slave. He and his fellows . . ." Blackbird pointed to slender poles from which floated the scalps of the unlucky Iroquois. "Let them whip poor will now," he said.

"I forgot to look for the war club," Half Sky began.

"You guided us and I'm going to tell your father so."

In silence they walked toward Herb Gatherer's tepee. Half Sky knew Blackbird did not intend to tell Crashing Thunder that his son had forgotten the magic club. Why should I tell Father the truth? he thought.

When they arrived at the medicine man's, Blackbird said, "Half Sky guided us. He . . ."

"Father," the boy interrupted, "I am not half so brave as you think me. I forgot to look for Grandfather's magic club. Perhaps it was lying right there. I was not smart at all. I just lost my head when I saw Mother and White Goose. I've failed on my first war party."

Herb Gatherer glanced at Crashing Thunder, who was watching Half Sky.

"I'm not as brave or as smart as Mother," the boy went on. "If she had not put the sleep powder in the stew, well, I don't know what would have happened."

"Well, she did put the sleep powder in, didn't she?" Crashing Thunder smiled. "And you found her. You did well, Half Sky."

Just then Flying Cloud came into the tepee. "You must come home, my husband, and see the new house we have."

"My wife, you are a smart squaw." Crashing Thunder looked happy and proud. "I will come if you promise you won't put any sleep powder in my stew," he teased. "You should wear the eagle feather."

"I?" Flying Cloud laughed. "No feather for me. Too easy to fool men. I did nothing much. Herb Gatherer gave me the powder for you when you got your shoulder hurt. I knew I'd have a use for it some day. Now, who wants to come and have some blueberry bread and corn soup?"

CHAPTER 13

Getting Ready for the Great Feast

HALF SKY lay on his bearskin looking at Flying Cloud. Now and then he thought how terrible everything had been when his mother was captured; then he opened his eyes wide and grinned when he saw her stirring the cooking pot. How her black hair shone! But why, he wondered, now that he was safe, did she look so sad? Through half-opened eyelids he watched her.

She sat poking the fire absently. Now and then she stirred the venison stew in the cooking pot. At times she held the long wooden spoon in the air. Once she started to rake out the white ashes with the spoon. She caught herself just in time and jerked the spoon back from the fire. She glanced at Half Sky and shook her head.

Just then Crashing Thunder came into the cabin. Flying Cloud's eyes brightened. "You're almost well, aren't you?" she asked.

"How your hair shines," he said as he put his hand on her shoulder. "But, Flying Cloud, what is troubling you? You can't fool me. Out with it. What's the matter?"

"It's—it's about Half Sky . . ."

"Half Sky?" Crashing Thunder looked toward his son.

"Why, there he sleeps like a bear in a hollow tree, fat as a raccoon. What ails him?"

"It's not what ails him. It's what ails his new clothes. Oh, his lovely new leggings I made! So long I hunted for porcupine quills to embroider them with. So far I walked to find the yellow dye plant. I saved the very nicest deerskin and tanned it with so much care. Oh dear, oh dear."

"Well . . ." Crashing Thunder patted her shoulder.

"And the long time I worked on his moccasins. On each I made the flaming hummingbird. Oh, dear, oh dear. And his earrings. And the beautiful white ear tufts. I just can't bear to think about them—all burned to a crisp."

"Oh, is that all?" Crashing Thunder filled the cabin with his booming laugh. He turned to Half Sky. "Get up, you fat porky, and tell your mother . . ."

"That nothing matters so long as we have you again," Half Sky finished for him. He walked over to his mother. "I don't care an empty gull's egg about new clothes. I don't care whether I wear any clothes. It doesn't matter."

Flying Cloud's sadness left. She laughed. "I'm afraid you would feel funny dancing around at the Great Feast without any clothes."

"I could paint myself," Half Sky suggested.

"Well, now, let's see what we can do," said Crashing Thunder. "What's the use of being chief if I can't figure out an answer to this?"

"Answer to what?" In the doorway stood Crow Tongue all smeared with wood ashes.

"Crow Tongue! Where have you been?" Flying Cloud asked.

"Where have I been, eh? Well, why do you think I've got ashes all over my face? I've been crying for my lost slave. Oh, I'm not mourning him. I'm just sorry for myself. Now I have to rustle wood and carry water. Oh, it was such a fine life while it lasted. I just snapped my fingers and said, 'Water or firewood, or pounded corn.' There it was like magic. Why couldn't you have brought that worthless Iroquois slave back to me to carry water and break up firewood?"

Crashing Thunder looked helplessly at Crow Tongue; then he beckoned to Half Sky. They both sneaked out toward the rock ledge.

"Your mother will handle Crow Tongue. Squaws! I don't understand them, Half Sky. But I'll wager my best bow against your best arrowhead that when we go back all the women in the village will be bringing in deerskins, hunting porcupine quills and dyeing them or doing beadwork on your moccasins. Your mother is a great manager. And you won't dance naked at the Great Feast."

Father and son walked to the smooth level spot beyond their cabin where men were inspecting the poles that stood ready to be covered with long strips of birch bark.

"We haven't much time to get this Big House ready for the Great Feast," Red Hawk said. "I wonder, Half Sky, if you and Big Face can go to the forest and get six saplings to replace these broken ones?"

Half Sky took his sharpest flint ax and found one for Big Face. The two boys ran off.

"Here comes Herb Gatherer." Crashing Thunder pointed to the medicine man, who was carrying in his hands all that was left of the mide drum after the fire—a smoked and partly charred piece of cedar log about sixteen inches long. The mide drum was the one that beat out the tribe's prayers, sorrows, and joys. Ojibways believed this drum carried within itself the welfare of the tribe. A terrible misfortune if it were destroyed.

"The mide drum. The mide drum," everybody said. "What will we do?"

"Now, don't get excited," Herb Gatherer said. He sat down by Crashing Thunder. "Our Father Drum has had a hard time, but perhaps I can doctor him up again."

"Hah! Good," everyone said. Word that Father Drum was to be repaired spread through the village, and all the warriors crowded about.

With his flint knife, Herb Gatherer scraped the charred wood from the log, then scoured the surface with sand. "Not hurt as much as I feared," he remarked. "Now, Chief, comes the ticklish part of putting on a new head. We'll have to pray to Father Drum." He held up his hand. Everyone stopped talking.

"Father Drum," Herb Gatherer began, "because of those Iroquois snakes who tried to kill you by burning, your head and your bottom were so hurt that we must give you a new head and bottom. I will be as careful as I can, but if I hurt you, I ask pardon. May it please you, Father Drum, to put all the old songs back under your new head.

"Our drummers are sad. They fear lest the old songs of our people were burned in the fire and will never again cheer and stir our tribe. Surely, you, O Father Drum, are stronger than the rascally Iroquois. Show us that you forgive any bungling we have done to you and tell us you are no longer sick but well and powerful."

Herb Gatherer scraped off the old charred head, the smoked porcupine quills, and the ruined leather bottom and thongs.

"Here, Red Hawk," he ordered, "give these parts of Father Drum honorable burial."

Crashing Thunder handed Herb Gatherer a new piece of well-cured buckskin and the two men carefully stretched it over the head of the drum. Then, while West Wind held the head, Herb Gatherer and Crashing Thunder stretched another piece of buckskin on the bottom. Herb Gatherer bound head and bottom together with a thong wound around the middle of the drum. One tiny piece of beadwork and a slightly scorched thunderbird made of porcupine quills he put back on the drum. West Wind brought new dyed porcupine quills to be arranged around the great thunderbird. These Herb Gatherer bound on the drum.

He painted the head half blue and half red. Between the red and blue parts he drew a thick yellow line. "O Father Drum," he said, "here is the blue, the upper sky; the red is the lower sky. The yellow is the path the sun takes."

Herb Gatherer examined the drum beater carefully. "Ah," he said, "it's all sound. A little scouring and it's as good as it ever was."

Finally Herb Gatherer called the head drummer to strike the drum. As the familiar "Bong, bong, bong," sounded, everyone rushed up and put a small present by the drum— a bead or two, bits of tobacco, colored porcupine quills.

Crashing Thunder gave the head drummer a string of sea shells, brought at great trouble from the Great Water.

Herb Gatherer then told the people they should often think of Father Drum and leave him presents so he would know he was not forgotten. "Ingratitude," Herb Gatherer said, "is something the Spirit of the Drum finds hard to forgive." He then asked again that Father Drum put back all the old songs so the people would not be lonesome.

At a sign from the medicine man each warrior came up, hit the drum once, and made a wish. They danced about, for they knew they would get what they had asked Father Drum to give them. Now Herb Gatherer picked up Father Drum and carried him inside the Big House where West Wind, the Keeper of the Drum, was sitting. Not until the end of the Great Feast would Father Drum be left alone.

After the warriors were satisfied that the operation on Father Drum was successful, they began to place the rolls of birch bark on the roof of the new building. As soon as they had finished, three squaws, keepers of the Big House, began to carry in dry grass for the people to sit on.

"Hah," these keepers called as they flounced along with their arms full of grass. "Hah! Look at those three men keepers of the Big House. They squat around all day and let us women get the place ready."

The three men keepers shook their long wands of office and retorted, "Hah. Ugh. Give a squaw a little say-so and see what happens."

"We want to know," the women began, "where you men keepers of the Big House stored those rolls of birch bark that are supposed to make a roof? Where the porcupines could gnaw holes in them and woodpeckers drill them to powder? Look! Like a sieve. Suppose it rains. Hah!"

Everyone began to laugh at the three men, for sure enough the birch-bark roof had many holes. Some boys chanted, "Keepers of the Big House, one, two, three. Keepers of the Big House. Hee! Hee! Hee!" And they began to run in and out of the Big House and point to the roof.

The women keepers scolded the boys and threatened to call Herb Gatherer. The squaws felt no one should find fault with the keepers except one who was a keeper.

By that night the Big House was ready for the morrow's celebration and the three keepers of the Big House sat at the doorway like carved images. Inside, the head drummer guarded Father Drum. Ever since the chief's cabin had burned, everyone was watchful and a little nervous. Children tried to peek inside, but the men keepers waved their wands and said, "G-r-r-r, G-r-r-r!"

Crashing Thunder, Half Sky, and Big Face went to the sweat house. It was barrel shaped like a huge drum, covered with roof mats and bearskins. Inside lay twelve enormous stones heated red hot, and near by were bark pails of water. Every now and then Crashing Thunder went in and sprinkled the stones with just enough water to make a dense steam. When the hut was filled with steam, Half Sky, his father, and Big Face went in. Sweat poured from their bodies. The boys thought they would suffocate. Their eyes were blurred, and to make matters worse, Crashing Thunder dropped several pinches of tobacco on the hot stones. The white smoke of the tobacco rose like the fog on their own Birch Island. Thicker and hotter the steam got, and just as Half Sky and

Big Face thought they could not stay another minute, Crashing Thunder raised the skin door curtain and told the boys to jump into the cold water of the bay.

When the icy water first touched Half Sky, he thought he couldn't move, but he soon began to swim and felt the blood rush through his body. He dived and swam under water toward Big Face, then he grabbed his friend's legs and pulled him down. Immediately he swam away like a big pike and came up a little distance away.

He watched. Big Face did not come up. Half Sky dived down again and swam toward the place where Big Face should be. There among the twisty pickerel weeds he saw Big Face. He grabbed him and brought him to the rock ledge.

"Are you all right, Big Face? I thought I'd play a trick on you. Did you hit your head on a rock? Are you all right?"

"Half Sky! So it was you. Yes, I hit my head a little tunk, but it wasn't that. I was scared. I thought the evil spirit of the water had me. I couldn't move, I was so scared."

"I guess we're clean anyway, Big Face, so let's go up to our house and get supper. I am sure Mother has beans and corn cooking in a venison stew. She can really make a stew."

"I'll race you to the cabin," Big Face answered.

When the boys tumbled into the cabin, Flying Cloud filled Big Face's bowl and looked intently at him. "You haven't been swimming too long in the cold water, have you?"

"Oh, no. I didn't swim far enough," Big Face told her. He gave Half Sky a look warning him not to say more.

"Well, Half Sky," his mother said, "thanks to all the Bear Clan women, you don't have to go naked to the Great Feast

You have clothes. Herb Gatherer left word that you boys are to go to his tepee tonight to rehearse your songs and practice your dance steps."

As the boys walked together to Herb Gatherer's, Big Face said, "I'm scared, Half Sky. Think of dancing around the Big House and singing our songs with all the people watching. I sing like a crow. Suppose we make a mistake. How do we know when to shake the gourd rattle straight and when to shake it sidewise? I know I'll drop it or step on my feet and fall down."

"I'm just as nervous as you, Big Face. What I'm afraid of is forgetting my song. Wouldn't that be awful? The drummers are fussy, too, about people keeping in step."

When they reached Herb Gatherer's, they raised the doorway curtain, but no one said, "Nind ubimin. Nind ubimin."

"That's strange," Big Face said. "Usually when anyone leaves his tepee, he props a stick against the curtain to say to everyone that the house is locked up and the owner away."

"Well," Half Sky said, "Herb Gatherer said to come and here we are. We can wait." They sat down.

"Look." Big Face nudged Half Sky. "Look at the tepee shake. And listen. It sounds as if there were a dozen people in there all talking at once."

Whoever was talking stopped suddenly. The tepee no longer rocked about. They stared. "Nind ubimin, Nind ubimin," they heard. They got up slowly, raised the doorway flap and walked inside.

Herb Gatherer noticed their staring eyes and said, "I've been talking to my manito. He it is who gives me power to teach you boys. Now we will go out to that flat rock in the forest where we can practice." He set a stick up against his doorway curtain, and the three walked to a level outcrop surrounded by a screen of balsam and cedar.

"The first thing you have to learn is the dance step. It's this way." Herb Gatherer shuffled forward three steps, put his weight on his left foot, and shuffled forward again while he clapped his hands. "You must keep time with your hands to the beat of the drum. Now you dance. I'll clap."

It looked easy but when Half Sky and Big Face tried it, they were out of step with the clapping. Big Face did better than Half Sky. Hour after hour they worked until Herb Gatherer felt they could "dance at it" as he said.

"Big Face," he said, "you've got the hang of this dancing. You help Half Sky tonight after you go home. But now you must dance to the drum and shake your rattles at the same time." He handed each boy a gourd with several little stones inside. "Now," he ordered and began to clap.

Half Sky shook his sidewise. "No, Half Sky. Remember, shake sidewise only when you sing your song. When you dance without singing, shake your rattle upright. That's right. Keep time to the drum beats."

Finally Half Sky and Big Face satisfied Herb Gatherer.

"Now, Big Face, you go back to my tepee while I go over Half Sky's song with him. Then I'll rehearse you. It isn't right for either of you to hear the other's song before the Great Feast."

After Big Face left, Herb Gatherer looked very solemn and said, "Half Sky, pretend this is the Big House. That big white birch stump is the drummer. Now it is your turn to get up and dance over to the red post trimmed with downy feathers—let's pretend it's that balsam over to your right. All ready, are you?"

Half Sky nodded and swallowed once or twice.

"The Wekaun or priest will say, 'Tonight, Half Sky, who has lately been given a blessing and seen a vision on Dreamer's Rock, will sing his song as his grandfathers for a string of years have done on this Birch Island.'

"Then you must get up; be sure you have your rattle, and don't forget to shake it upright when you dance, sidewise when you sing. Now." Herb Gatherer began to hum and clap his hands.

Half Sky grasped his rattle and started to dance slowly toward the slender birch. "Now the priest will say, 'Who stands to help this young man?' Someone will get up and stand just behind you. Then you begin your song. Now let's hear it."

For a moment Half Sky had no idea what to say. He stood there foolishly shaking the rattle. "Come," said Herb Gatherer impatiently. "You are not so dumb as you look. Come, the song!"

Stung by Herb Gatherer's remark, Half Sky began in a squeaky voice:

> "We, your helpers, small but mighty
> Whirring round we all things see.
> Always near you when you need us,
> When you call we bring blessings."

"Again," ordered Herb Gatherer. "Try to shake your rattle harder. You are keeping in tune to the drum all right."

The second time Half Sky did so well Herb Gatherer said

he could rest. "And tonight eat enough so your voice will ring out good and clear. You want everybody to hear what you say."

"When I get through dancing at the Great Feast, what do I do?"

"Oh, you sit down on a cedar mat near the red post and the priest, the Wekaun, will give you good words and then you will see the megis, the mystery of our religion, the white sea shell from the Great Salt Water, the sign of everlasting life. It is the greatest moment of a warrior's life when he first sees the Me-da-nee-gis. You will never forget it."

Half Sky went to sit down and wait for his friend, and Herb Gatherer, wiping the sweat from his forehead, called Big Face. He listened to his song and advised him as he had Half Sky.

Then both boys went to their homes to rest and get ready for the feast the next day.

CHAPTER 14

Feather Dance

THE DAY of the Great Feast, Half Sky thought as he opened his eyes.

"Wake up, Half Sky," Crashing Thunder called to his son. "Don't you know you must bathe in the water of the bay? Don't you know this is the beginning of the Great Feast and you must be clean?"

"Oooh," Half Sky said, "those cold waters of the bay." He almost shivered, but he didn't, because that would be a disgrace. He followed his father, and they both jumped into the gray water. He was glad his father did not swim around more than a few minutes, for the water was just as cold as he had thought it would be.

When Crashing Thunder and Half Sky stepped out of the water, they walked slowly to the cabin. "Don't let anyone think we minded the cold water," Crashing Thunder advised. "Make believe it is a very hot day."

Flying Cloud had bowls of creamy whitefish soup and boiled beans ready, along with fresh baked bread and plenty of sweet bear oil. Half Sky stuffed himself as did Crashing Thunder who boomed out, "Oongh ondjita—that's what I like."

"When does the feast start?" Half Sky asked.

"Today we are going to have a surprise. At noon some warriors of a friendly tribe are coming to give their feather dance. They should be paddling up to the landing any minute now. They are the best jugglers and sleight-of-hand magicians I have ever seen. We Ojibways don't have a feather dance, so it will be fun to see it."

"H o-n e e—h o-n e e," Half Sky heard the hailing cry. "Father," he said, "there's a canoe coming in right now."

Crashing Thunder and Half Sky rushed to the landing place where two canoes were being pulled up on the shore. "The Wekaun, the priests and the feather dancers," the chief said.

All the children of Birch Island, it seemed, were crowding around the feather dancers, who smiled broadly and kept calling, "Ho! Ho! Ho!" The priests, thin older men, moved their arms about as if glad to get out of the crowded canoe. They sniffed the breakfast smells and nodded.

"Will it please you to come to my house?" Crashing Thunder asked. They all accepted.

Half Sky worried about the amount of fish soup his mother had. He ran ahead as fast as he could to tell her, but he needn't have worried, because there bubbled a cooking pot filled with that same delicious creamy fish soup.

He hurried back to look at the strangers. Big Face joined Half Sky, and the two boys stared at the priests and magicians.

"I wonder what that reedlike thing is one of the feather dancers is carrying," Half Sky said.

"You don't suppose he blows arrows out of it, do you?" said Big Face.

Just then the dancer put the long reed to his lips; the boys heard soft sweet music. "Like the south wind singing in the birch trees in the spring," Half Sky whispered. He decided he'd like to learn how to make that music.

Flying Cloud seemed to have cooking pots that could never be emptied because she fed all the strangers and still had soup left. Half Sky was proud when one of the priests said it was the best soup he had ever eaten.

Crashing Thunder, Half Sky and Big Face put up a tepee for the priests to dress in. Big Face hurried home to put on his new clothes, and Half Sky began to dress himself in his beautifully embroidered leggings. He especially admired the breechcloth trimmed with colored quills. His shoulder pocket to carry his deerskin medicine bag was beautiful, but the moccasins were gayest of all with hummingbirds made of colored beads on the toes.

When Crashing Thunder had painted Half Sky's face red and black and had readjusted the ear tufts of white down, he stepped back and looked at his son. "Hah," he said. "You'll do."

Big Face came in just then. "Oh." He stood staring at Half Sky. "Why—why—I hardly knew you. Do I look any-where near as fine as you do?"

Half Sky felt so choked in his throat he did not dare speak. He nodded. Both boys pretended that their new clothes did not interest them at all. However, they swaggered about the village.

"Oh look, Big Face," whispered Half Sky. "Look, there comes Little Perch. Wonder if she will know us?"

She did. She began to giggle and then rushed off. "Come and see the two dandies," she called to the other girls.

All at once the boys were the center of a circle of girls who giggled and whispered to one another. That was too much for Half Sky and Big Face, and they hurried back to the chief's house. Here they found Flying Cloud, White Goose, and Crashing Thunder all dressed up. Half Sky looked twice at his father, for the fluffy turkey-feather headdress made the chief look as tall as a pine tree. What a handsome man his father was, he thought.

After everyone had drunk a bowl of thin corn soup, Flying Cloud, White Goose, Half Sky, and Big Face went into the Big House. The chief must walk in the procession with the priests and dancers.

Inside the Big House the women of the Otter Clan sat nearest the door, next the Otter men. Across the room were the Muskrat women and next the Muskrat men. Flying Cloud's clan, the Bear, took places at the end of the hall. Of course Half Sky and White Goose went with Flying Cloud, because the children always belong to the mother's clan.

Big Face had to go to still another place, for he was a Caribou.

Suddenly a ripple of giggles started, and when Half Sky looked around to see what made the villagers laugh, he saw Crow Tongue with her face covered with black stripes.

"She's still mourning for her no-good Iroquois slave," Half Sky whispered.

Since Crow Tongue was also a Bear, she sat down next to Flying Cloud.

A drumbeat brought a sudden hush. The procession was coming in with Crashing Thunder at its head. Boom, boom, boom, went the drum and behind it, keeping step to the solemn tapping, walked the three men attendants of the Big House, each carrying a slender wand. Next marched the three women attendants with turkey wings. Now, whirling about, but still keeping time to the drumbeat, came the feather dance jugglers. After them the three flute players. Last of all marched the two tall and gaunt priests, the Wekauns.

Once to the north, once to the south, then to the east, then to the west went the procession. With a final boom of the drum, Crashing Thunder stopped as he reached the north end again. He flourished his war-club One-who-guards-and-warns-of-danger.

"Whee! Whee! Whee!" everyone chanted.

The priests sat down on their cedar mats. Crashing Thunder began to speak:

"We have a surprise for you. We have visitors from our great ally to the south, the noble Miamis. They will open the Great Feast with their feather dance. The Great Spirit has given them the power to make our hearts merry. That is the way the Great Spirit wants his children to be, happy. It is good."

Crashing Thunder took his place among his clan. The three feather dancers arose with great flappings of their loose white deerskin capes. A gasp went up from the villagers. The dancers looked like three gigantic white birds with huge wing spreads. Now and then the dancers threw their cloaks about wildly, and the crowd caught a glimpse of their bodies painted with brilliant colors. Half Sky noticed that they carried long slender poles with bunches of feathers on them. Now with white robes wrapped tightly about them, they bowed to the priests, to the chief. Suddenly the three flute players joined the white-caped ones, and through the Big House sounded the soft flute music, long drawn out and ending on a mournful note.

"The loon," Half Sky whispered.

"The loon, the loon!" the villagers shouted. While the attention of the audience had been centered on the musicians, the three jugglers had arranged their feather pompons so that they looked for all the world like loons. Black and white, these tufts of feathers seemed to turn into loons floating in air just as they had rocked quietly in the blue water around Birch Island all summer long.

"Ah—ooo— ah—ooo— ah—ooo!" The flutes sounded exactly as the loons call in the twilight.

As suddenly as the sad cry began, it ceased. "Ha-ha-ha-ha," the flutes began again. The drummers joined in with sharp, quick, high notes, tap, tappy, tap, tap, tap.

"Ha-ha-ha-ha," the jugglers laughed and kept tune with flutes and drums.

The dancers made the black and white feathers jump high in the air. They rolled over one another, they collided. Over and over and over they rose and fell to the shrill trilling ha-ha-ha of the jugglers, while the flutes tremoloed and the drummers beat short gay notes.

"Just exactly like those crazy loons," Half Sky whispered. The delighted villagers watched for a time in silence, then a great roar went up. Suddenly without anyone's seeing how the dancers did it, the loons had changed to huge wide-winged horned owls. They swooped softly about and pretended to grab White Goose. They chattered their beaks to the time of the drums. Now the owls fought one another, and feathers flew about the Big House. Then they stopped fighting and swooped about and pounced on Big Face's bare toes. Children screamed and the onlookers roared. "Ho, ho, ho," they yelled. "The great horned one is good."

The dancers sank to the floor with capes wrapped about them. The flute players put their instruments to their lips. Tootle-te-tootle-te-tootle they whistled. "A woodpecker," Half Sky said. Heetle-tee-heetle-tee-heetle, the flutes answered.

Suddenly woodpeckers fluttered from under the jugglers' deerskin capes. "Tap, tappity, tap," the dancers said. Tap, tappity, tap, from the drums, Heetle-tee-heetle-tee-heetle from the flutes. So real was it that several warriors looked up at the roof. The dancers dashed here and there until it seemed the Big House was alive with woodpeckers looking for bugs.

After the applause died down and quiet came, a single flutist played new notes. "Whip poor will! Whip poor will!" The feathers on the dancers' wands turned into whippoorwills.

But that was not the end. Ducks quacked scoldings; trumpeter swans sounded their cries like great bells ringing and horns tooting high up in the sky. Red-winged blackbirds sang, crows cawed hoarsely, gulls screamed. Every bird that had ever nested on Birch Island appeared. Half Sky saw them; he heard them.

Finally all three flutists repeated the loon's Ha-ha-ha, Ah-ooo, the great horned owl's chattering and his deadly who—oo who—oo, and the woodpecker's whistle. Then white ducks quacked and blackbirds sang, the drums gave out a grand skirl, and all was still. No one had seen the flutists and dancers disappear. They were gone.

Crashing Thunder got up and, after bowing to the priests, thanked the flutists, the drummers, and the feather dancers. He announced that the real Great Feast would open at sundown.

CHAPTER 15

Great Feast

IT WAS not until the next afternoon that Half Sky woke up. He grinned as he lay on his bearskin bed, for outside he heard Crow Tongue scolding.

"Of all things, for everyone to be talking about those silly bird dancers. I could do just as well myself. All they did was to fool us. That's the way. Some silly billy comes from another tribe and performs a few antics . . ."

Half Sky heard his father chuckle and his mother laugh. Gradually Crow Tongue's words grew fainter. "She must have gone on, so I'll get up," Half Sky said.

His father stuck his head inside the cabin. "It's about time you got up, lazybones. The sun is getting low, and you have to get a sweat bath. If you don't hurry, I'll eat all the supper. Remember it's a sweat bath before you eat."

Outside Half Sky found Big Face waiting, and both boys wished they were coming out instead of going into the sweat house. Inside, the steam seemed denser than they had ever seen it. "Sweat is right," Big Face said. "The water is just pouring down me."

"If I stay here much longer," Half Sky gasped, "I'll be so small my new clothes won't fit."

At last the boys decided they were clean and together they jumped into the icy waters of the bay. Their teeth chattered as they swam up to the landing place and hustled out. "See you later," each called as he ran home to eat.

Flying Cloud's hot corn bread and the savory stew of wild duck, venison and squash set the blood tingling in Half Sky's body. He dressed in his new clothes and was relieved that he hadn't melted quite away. Flying Cloud and White Goose put on white doeskin skirts and blouses and beautifully fringed leggings and embroidered moccasins.

Crashing Thunder wore his fluffy turkey-feather headdress and carried the club, One-who-guards-and-warns-of-danger. He did not go with Half Sky, Flying Cloud, and White Goose because again he must walk in the procession with the priests.

As the evening before, the men and women sat separately, otter, caribou, muskrat, and bear clans together. Everyone was quiet, because today was a religious day, not just fun like the night before. Soon the drum began its booming.

The procession marched four times around the Big House and stopped at the north end where a little platform had been built. The women attendants brushed this off with their turkey wings and the priests sat down. Crashing Thunder went to sit with his own clan.

Tonight two small fires had been built in the Big House, one at the north end and one at the south. The red glare as it played over nodding crests, feather shawls, painted bodies, bead necklaces and red, green, blue, and white earrings, fascinated Half Sky. Everything was entirely different from yesterday. Even the drum had a different tone, deep and sad,

Half Sky thought, like the Bell Rocks when Grandfather
Footsteps of the Bear struck them with One-who-guards-and-
warns-of-danger.

The older priest now stood up.

"Great Spirit," he prayed, "Master of everything visible
and invisible, Master of all spirits good and bad, be so kind as
to order the good spirits to help your children, the Ojibways.
Order the bad ones to keep away. Keep the strength of our
warriors. Keep the old persons in health so they may give of
their wisdom to the young. Keep our children. May they live
to be old, and above all, be happy. Give us a seedtime and a
harvest. Provide plenty of beasts in the forests for us to eat.
From all surprise attacks of the enemy deliver us, Great
Spirit. And when it is our time to go to the Land of Souls,
send us safely there over the narrow bridge that we may see
again our fathers, mothers, wives, husbands, and children.
Hear our voice, Great Spirit." He sat down.

The second priest arose.

"Take heart, my brethren. How great are the works of the
Great Spirit. Let us cheer up. We shall conquer our enemies,
our corn yield will be good. We shall be in good health. The
Ojibways shall prosper." He sat down.

The first priest stood up. "I welcome you all," he said, "all
who have come to worship. Tonight Blackbird will be your
leader and may the Great Spirit give him strength to do his
work. Sparrow Hawk will help him."

The drum sounded three times. Blackbird and Sparrow
Hawk walked slowly to the platform. They shook their gourd
rattles. The drummer struck the drum again three times.
Blackbird, still shaking his rattle, began to dance the length

of the Big House while the drummer sounded a monotonous song.

Blackbird sang of how he found the bead dropped by Flying Cloud and so tracked the Iroquois.

When he finished, Sparrow Hawk and the drummer repeated his words, and the others hummed the tune Blackbird had used. Then Herb Gatherer arose and, after saying, "I must worship," he told how his manito had come in a rushing wind and had advised that he get Rolling Eyes. He, too, danced the length of the Big House and the drummer repeated his words.

As Herb Gatherer sat down, Half Sky saw several women go out. He wondered why they left, but soon he heard cooking pots clattering. The women were going to bring in food.

Next West Wind began, "I must worship," and told his vision and sang about his helper. He used a funny jerky tune and words that went like this:

> "No *fish biting, not a one*
> *Cooking pots empty, all at once*
> *Nets all empty, empty all.*
> *On the shore away from home*
> *Came my helper in a storm*
> *Wings aflutter showing kindness.*"

Again the drummer repeated the words. Half Sky decided his helper must be a sea gull. At least the manito had brought fish. He was still thinking about West Wind's vision when he heard the priest say, "We have two young men who have had their first visions. They have found their helpers."

Blackbird said, "Who will help the young man, Half Sky?"

"I will," said Sparrow Hawk.

Half Sky was so scared he could hardly get up. Slowly he walked toward the platform. What was he going to do? He couldn't remember one word of his song. He would shake his rattle and dance as he had been told, he thought. Somehow one of his feet stepped on the other and his moccasin came part way off. He could see people around him trying not to laugh. What would he do if he couldn't remember the words?

Sparrow Hawk came up behind him. "I must worship," he prompted. "Say it—'I must worship.'"

"I must worship," Half Sky repeated in a faint voice.

Then he thought of how Footsteps of the Bear would feel if his grandson were to forget his song. Suddenly he heard a whirring of tiny wings. He remembered the words of his song.

> "We, your helpers, small but mighty
> Whirring round we all things see;
> Always near you when you need us,
> When you call, we bring blessings."

The drummers caught the rhythm and tapped it out as they repeated the song.

Half Sky caught a glimpse of his father's face. How glad he was he had remembered the song.

"Shake your rattle upright now," Sparrow Hawk whispered. "Dance toward the platform."

Half Sky saw many warriors get up and join in the dance. His fear left him. He had a helper who was to be relied on. Hadn't he heard the hummingbird when he thought he had forgotten his song? Great waves of thankfulness swept over

Suddenly he remembered the words of his song

him. Truly the Great Spirit was very near and making Himself known.

At last he had danced around the Big House, and he sat down with his bear clan. His mother nodded and smiled. Even Crow Tongue was pleased.

Now it was Big Face's turn.

"Who will help this young man?" he heard the priest say.

"I will," Crashing Thunder answered and took his place behind Big Face. Poor Big Face, thought Half Sky. I know just how he feels. At least Big Face didn't step on his own feet and almost fall. I wonder what his song is.

"I must worship," Big Face began in a voice almost as quavery as Half Sky's had been. Then he went on:

> *"Laughing, calling on the water,*
> *Smarter far than people think,*
> *We will help you with your fishing,*
> *Call us and we'll bring you blessing."*

"Oh, so that's it," Half Sky said, then was afraid someone had heard him. But nobody paid attention to anything except Big Face's song. Everyone was guessing who his helper was. Big Face had said something about being a fish caller.

The priest said, "How did your helper tell you to call the fish, my son?"

"He said to stand by the shore before anyone started to fish and say, 'O ye fishes, listen to my words. Let yourselves be caught by us. We will honor you. We will never burn your bones but bury them honorably.' "

"This village has been without a fish caller for a time. Now the Great Spirit has given you Big Face. I now name him

Official Fish Caller. You will see to it, Big Face, that no bones of our brothers, the fish, are burned. They must be buried. Never must more fish be caught than the people can use. Never must fish be taken and allowed to spoil. The Great Spirit gave the fish; now He has made you their protector."

The drummer repeated the song and Big Face danced in perfect time to the music. Half Sky was proud of him and proud, too, of Crashing Thunder who, tall and dignified, danced behind his friend.

Next Flying Cloud sang her song about how in the darkness of early morning the Iroquois pushed her into the canoe and took her away. She told how she prayed to her helper and was given the idea of putting the make-sleep powder in the stew so her captors' senses were dulled, and she was rescued. Many villagers heard the story for the first time and scarcely breathed as Flying Cloud told of her trick.

Half Sky watched Crashing Thunder and saw how proud he was of his wife. He thanked the Great Spirit that he had parents who were so fond of each other.

Now the women brought in cooking pots which they set down every few feet. Everyone filled his bowl with the corn soup. Half Sky's clan told him how well he had done and congratulated him on his helper. Big Face looked over at his friend and winked. Half Sky gave thanks to the Great Spirit for a friend like Big Face.

After the corn had been eaten, and the cooking pots taken out, the second priest got up.

"Now we will give thanks to the Great Spirit and pray for continued blessings," he said.

"Hooo, hooo, hooo," everyone said twelve times.

They all got up and danced the length of the Big House. They touched the center pole on which Half Sky saw the club, One-who-guards-and-warns-of-danger. They all sat down again and the first priest said:

"We must pray. *From fire and deluge,*"

"*Great Spirit deliver us. Hoo, Hoo, Hoo,*" the people replied.

"*From sudden disgraceful death and hurt from evil spirits,*"

"*Great Spirit deliver us,*" the people again replied.

"*From famine, sickness and witchcraft,*"

"*Great Spirit deliver us,*" ended the Great Feast.

The women brought in broiled venison, broiled fish, and sweet corn cakes. Everyone visited and stuffed himself. What food was left Blackbird gave to widows and widowers. A woman passed around some sea shells and everyone took one to remember the feast by.

The two priests thanked Blackbird and Sparrow Hawk and the attendants, and gave the final blessing. Half Sky knew that no one was happier than he. His mother and father were proud of him. He had a friend in Big Face as long as they should live. Best of all, he had found his manito; he had experienced the peace and blessing of the Great Spirit which would abide with him forever.